The Stand-In

The Stand-In

David Helwig

The Porcupine's Quill

NATIONAL LIBRARY OF CANADA
CATALOGUING IN PUBLICATION DATA

Helwig, David, 1938–
    The stand-in / David Helwig.

ISBN 0-88984-244-2

    I. Title.

PS8515.E4S83 2002   C813'.54   C2002-902158-8
PR9199.3.H445S83 2002

1 2 3 4 • 04 03 02

Published by The Porcupine's Quill, www.sentex.net/~pql
68 Main Street, Erin, Ontario NOB ITO.

Represented in Canada by the Literary Press Group.
Trade orders are available from University of Toronto Press.

We acknowledge the support of the
Ontario Arts Council, and the Canada
Council for the Arts for our publishing
program. The financial support of the
Government of Canada through the
Book Publishing Industry
Development Program is also
gratefully acknowledged.

ONTARIO ARTS COUNCIL
CONSEIL DES ARTS DE L'ONTARIO

Canadä

The Canada Council | Le Conseil des Arts
for the Arts | du Canada

to the listeners

One

It is death brought me here, ladies and gentlemen. I am not the man you wanted, but Denman Tarrington, who had been invited to deliver this first set of Jakeson lectures, is no longer with us. A week ago he was found dead on a green tile floor in front of a mirror covered with steam in a hotel near Lincoln Centre. As a result of that – misadventure let us call it – your committee had to find a replacement with words at the ready and prepared to come to a small Canadian campus in the depth of winter. I am told that a Famous Feminist declined. A Great Scholar pleaded illness. And so it went, until I walked into my apartment in Montreal one evening, after an absence of a few days, and the telephone rang. A proposal was made to me. As a retired professor who taught for many years at this institution, I could be assumed to be prepared for the weather, and so yesterday afternoon, a small plane dropped out of the clouds into a snowsquall, and I was driven through the white sweep of empty land and delivered to you as a last desperate gesture to avoid annulment.

We don't care what you say as long as you fill three hours. That is what I have been told. In words almost that blunt. Since I delivered lectures here for nearly forty years, it was felt I could be counted on. Yes, and when I left, I mentioned to one or two colleagues research subjects I intended to pursue in my retirement, a gesture conventional enough, but remembered by someone, I suppose.

Your president, when he introduced me, gave a brief and kind though somewhat inaccurate account of my career, but it is perhaps as well to let it stand. You will not remember corrections if I offer them, though I am compelled to say that I was not a championship badminton player, even when I was a hard-muscled and competitive young man. I will admit to a fondness for the game, but Denman Tarrington, who had long arms and a quick way of slicing the bird into a difficult corner, often defeated me, though in doubles my wife and I could drive him and his tall consort into the floor of the court. The late Denman Tarrington, as we must now refer to him. For most of you he is only a name, a celebrated, semi-divine figure who left this university before you arrived, before some of you were born.

I remember once meeting him in the corridor of Arminian Hall on his way to teach a class, when he stopped to explain to me how much he liked going in to lecture with the musk of a female student fresh in his beard. That was many years ago, of course, when teachers were allowed to treat their classes as a harem, although I'm not sure the Baptist elders on the Board of Governors ever gave their explicit approval. Still it was the way of the times and Tarrington was quick to sense possibilities. I imagine he was also quick to sense that the world had changed and he might have to stop.

Though he garbled a few things in his introduction, your president — and I am grateful to you, sir — got the title of my lecture series correct. 'The Music of No Mind.' Appropriate perhaps to mention at this point that I believe the title is a quotation, though I have been unable to locate the source. Yesterday evening, I spent an hour at the university library trying to run it down, but I failed, though I did overhear a conversation, which was not without interest, on the subject of tattoos and where on her perfect body a young woman might have one inscribed. The students who were discussing the matter were disgusted by nose rings. As I am myself. Some of you may be aware of Tarrington's little book, *Body Piercing and Theories of Transcendence*. The picture on the back cover shows Tarrington with a ring in his nose. Old bull that he was.

The Music of No Mind. What that means will become clear, I trust, as the series of lectures goes on, but it strikes me now that the errors in your president's introduction of me are indeed germane. I have corrected one, but will not correct them all, and from this day the errors will take on the nature of fact. What is spoken must be, in some sense, true. Did you know that the finest artist this country has produced was listed in an important exhibition catalogue as deceased several months before his death, and that even years later, many argued for the catalogue's veracity?

Beside me, on the table that holds my glass of water, you will see a book which is that artist's biography. The liquid in the glass, let me say, is water, though had Denman Tarrington survived his last hot wash to stand here, it would no doubt have been gin or vodka. After one or two youthful adventures, I made the decision to abstain from alcohol, and in earlier years this was held against me. I must be a cissy, since I didn't get drunk with the boys. When Tarrington, in his days on this campus, wasn't tampering with his female students, he was often to be found carrying on an uproarious and wide-reaching unofficial seminar in a local dive. Occasionally I would drop in – we were friends, at least of a sort – and now and then I would make my small contribution to the discussion. Once or twice, I believe, Tarrington or one of his students arranged to have my soft drink spiked. I hope I survived the evenings with my dignity intact. Memory is vague, but I believe on those nights there were more than the usual number of jokes in questionable taste. The world has grown more abstemious now. Once, drink was everyone's muse. No more. Now they are all dead or on the wagon.

The history of history: look here, inside the cover of my copy of this biography, a number of abrupt communications which have been placed there with a rubber stamp. In an assertive red we are told that the book is *Property of Maritime Air Command*. At some point in its history – letters also in red but in a different typeface tell us – it belonged to the *Maritime Air Command Station Library, Gorsebrook*. Just below these two messages are those saddest, saddest words of all, rubber-stamped twice in a sort of rusty orange, *Library Discard*, and below, again, yet paler, *Library Discard*. So it came into my hands in a second-hand book shop in Halifax, though there is a name in greasy blue ballpoint ink which suggests I was not the first owner after the Maritime Air Command had abandoned it.

Of course we ask ourselves questions about the book, who it was in Maritime Air Command who read it, and whether – it was published in 1936 – it might have been the favoured reading of a young pilot who hoped to become a painter but later went down over the Atlantic or in Germany. In the lower corner of the blank page before the half-title, there is one more imprint of a rubber stamp, in purple this time. *With the Compliments of the Canadian Committee, 56 Sparks Street, Ottawa.* So this, we must guess, is how the book came into the Station Library at Gorsebrook. A few patriots in Ottawa, determined that men in the armed forces should be made aware of the art of their country, sent it off.

The cast of characters in Ottawa: in a good but slightly worn suit, a man of middle age who until recently had difficulty finding work, but has now got a place with the Canadian Committee and who reads through the publishers' lists in search of books that might be sent out to sailors, soldiers and airmen. Giving this man his marching orders, the chairman of the organization, a short broad person who has made his living as a lawyer, one with many political connections and a surprising streak of idealism as well as a powerful dislike of the United States. He is reputed to be the slave of his shrewish wife, but that is a misunderstanding of their relationship, for in fact they are fond of each other, and if he listens to her opinions, it is because he respects them. There were, of course, others involved in the committee, but they are no business of ours. One of the men we have met was aware of the work of James Wilson Morrice and felt that copies of the first biography should be bought and distributed.

All this is less than perfectly certain, you will say, but the imprints of those stamps are there in the front of the book. Here, if I hold it up, you can see them. There, you see, *Library Discard, Library Discard,* stamped twice with the energy of some inchoate anger by one of those librarians whose most urgent desire is to throw things out. The unofficial editor set loose in the book of life. Here in the corner is the stamp of the Canadian Committee, those two men in Ottawa.

This biography I hold in my hand comes from the days when it was still possible to write a life without a thousand footnotes. Such a book would now be twice as long, swollen with attributions. Here we have only a prefatory note explaining who it was the author spoke with when he set out to tell his tale. He was, of course, writing when those who had known his subject were still alive, including Somerset Maugham, whose work I admired in the days before he was consigned to the junkheap. Hard to believe now, but I met Maugham once, in a restaurant near Menton, though I spoke only a few words, and he was silent, a wrinkled, stone-eyed old creature with the face of a snapping turtle, basking in the sun of the Riviera, hating the world. Memory and hate: the two are twins.

Let us look at two moments, many years apart, each of them, perhaps, indicative. In 1905, Maugham was in France, and he got to know Morrice as one of the artists who dined in a restaurant in Montparnasse called Le Chat Blanc, in an upstairs room where a number of artists and literary figures gathered. This was La Belle Époque, when Paris was the centre of the world. In one of his novels, Maugham described the painter, a man with a shining bald pate, pointed beard, bright exophthalmic eyes, drunk. Maugham would have it, in his portrait of Morrice under another name, that he was frequently so shaky from drink that his hand could hardly hold a brush. The biographer tells us that while Maugham perhaps exaggerates the painter's alcoholism, he was known to sit in the cafés with his little box of paints, drinking absinthe, doing those small rapid brilliant oil sketches – on thin pieces of wood – of whatever he saw in front of his chair at the café, perhaps close by his apartment on the Quai des Grands Augustins, only a few steps from where Picasso, who had arrived in Paris months before, set up a studio some years later.

So there we have Morrice, as portrayed by Maugham, inebriated, popular, a man of whom no one had a bad word to say.

Well then, we move forward to 1961. Just like that. One quick cut. We all live in the movies now. Morrice is long dead. The clothes the actors wear are different, of course, the furnishings, the quality of the light. We are at Maugham's villa, not very far from the restaurant where I saw the ancient reptile. He is well on in years, and on this evening, he has grown weary and abandoned his company, including his daughter, and retired to his room where he has fallen into a state of agitation. The old brain is failing, and a primitive rage is set loose. 'I will show them,' he shouts, or so we are told. 'I'll put them back into the gutter where they belong. I'll get even with them. Sons of bitches!' The man who was his secretary and lover gave him a sedative and he lapsed into sleep and silence.

I will have more to say about silence. The phone rings. No one there.

Biography is a curious discipline. No secret that the selection of incidents allows the story to be told in any number of ways. If the subject wrote or spoke, the bias of his own statements will create the framework which is filled in by the later babblers. Of course, in nearly every case, the subject of a biography is celebrated. It is clear that fame has its own narrative, and the public achievements must be the justification of any life's telling.

Say that I was to write a biography of our colleague, Denman Tarrington. That phrase – our colleague – is merely conventional, of course, since few of you knew him. I do see Frank Puncheon and Annabelle Disney among you. Yes, Belle, I noticed your presence and those perfect new teeth. Did you notice mine? *Ou sont les dents d'antan?* You of course knew Denman when I did. I remember things he said about you, though I won't repeat them right now. We can meet later.

Perhaps I am out of the habit of giving lectures. I notice – as I shouldn't – the faces in front of me, Annabelle of the Perfect Teeth, your ruddy president, several with their eyes closed who may be contemplating my words or, more likely, have simply dozed off. There are three men with striped neckties. Now the necktie is growing more unusual everywhere, even in the academic world, and to see three striped ones in this audience is odd almost to the point that one might consider it ominous. Three members of a Certain Department. Three strips of stripes from the drunken brush of God.

To return: say I was to set out to biographize DT. The justification would not be that my wife and I trounced him and Madeleine on the badminton court. Who would wish to know such a thing, or any of the other events of our young lives that were shared here on nights when snow howled round the house, except that *our* Denman went on to become *their* Denman, the public intellectual, coming forth from his small New England college to define the symbols of contemporary life in those famous, and if I may say so, incoherent essays like 'Happy Electron Bombardment' and 'The Suicide Note as a Rhetoric of Desire'? I would be compelled to search for the roots of his informing ideas on the badminton court or in the dark nights of snowbound endurance or to tell shaggy anecdotes of what came later, how his wife vanished, how my wife became his.

Every generation has its own language. To catch Tarrington's essence, one would have had to catch the tone, half learned, half vulgar, of his speech. Maugham's biographer, if I may make a quick step back for a flick-of-the-wrist drop shot, points out that he was in his manner of speech essentially an Edwardian, a fusty old party who habitually used the phrase 'sexual congress' for an activity he was fond of. With both sorts, it appears, but mostly with chaps. Morrice had a pretty French mistress. That was how things were then.

I may say, Mr President, that it had been my hope to illustrate this lecture with slides, but in my race to the airport in Montreal, I left the box of slides in a taxicab, and though I will attempt to trace them, it is possible that I will never see them again, and I must create the required images by means of words. I would not disparage the power of language, but have you ever tried to find words for colour, green, let us say? We have that one word, and so we are driven to likenesses, metaphors. There are all the vegetable greens, the green of a stick of celery, the green of a pepper squash, the green, not very different perhaps, of spinach, the green of the avocado, unknown in Canada in my youth but now so common, the green of unripe pears, unripe apples, leaves in bud and the mosses and fungi, all the greens of green. My daughter married a man named Green, and I have Green grandchildren. There was too the hint of green in the skin of the great DT as he lay dead on the floor of that New York hotel, blood no longer circulating, the skin first pale, then growing discoloured and under the fluorescent lights showing that slightest tendency to the pallor verdurous.

Then there are Morrice's greens and hints of green. I was speaking of Maugham, who as a young man couldn't see the point of the Impressionists. Though he collected paintings later on, some of them valuable, we can't take him seriously as an art critic, but it's worth noting he says of his fictionalized Morrice that he has the most fascinating sense of colour in the world. If one were to examine the small painting of a juggler entertaining a crowd on a street by the Seine, one would say that the predominant colours are black and certain tones of ochre, the juggled balls highlights of red, and yet there is everywhere a feeling of green or blue or conversation between the two. I revived my memory of all these things in your library just this morning. The river is brown but not quite brown, for like the Seine itself, it has a dim green transparency. In an earlier, smaller, quicker oil sketch, a Paris street with a kiosk, there is a sense of the light of evening, and in the darkening background, against a sky that is mauve with touches of yellow ochre, once again, hints of some odd green. If one examined his work side by side with the Impressionists who were still painting around him, or even the *intimistes* like Bonnard and Vuillard, one might say that he was the prince of greens. The manner of his famous painting looking outward from a café in Cuba is in ways parallel to that of his friend Matisse, but the colours, green orchestrated against yellow and blue, would have been alien to Matisse.

You take my point, patient while I sip my water, and of course some of you will wonder whether I told the truth, whether there may not be a little vodka or a touch of gin. No, of course not, though we all know that while speech and truth may sleep in the same bed, they never marry.

Madeleine drank vodka. If we went to their house after a badminton game, she would sometimes take a bottle of vodka out of the freezer, pour some, put a little pepper on top and drink it down. In an emergency – and there were emergencies, but that was in another age – she drank it warm. After three drinks she became vague and slack and easy. It was a kind of happiness, I suppose.

Battledore and shuttlecock, that's what the game was called originally, or perhaps that was the name of the children's sport that was the origin of badminton, named, we are told, for the country estate of the duke of Beaufort where it is supposed to have originated around 1873. J. W. Morrice, our prince of all the greens, was then eight years old, a schoolboy in Montreal, attending school in a building which is now the site of the Ritz Carlton, where I eat from time to time.

Badminton was the favourite form of exercise of another of the great Edwardians, H. G. Wells. Some of you will have heard the story of the pleasant odour of Wells's skin, how he smelt like honey and though odd-looking, was irresistible to women. There are men like that, blessed by the gods, while the rest of us are judged by our behaviour. Madeleine told me that Tarrington's skin smelled like fresh-cut hay.

They were an oddly assorted lot, the Edwardians, Wells, with his honey skin, Maugham trying to hide his inversion, Bennett, like Maugham a stammerer, making himself a writer out of sheer vulgar determination. They were between two worlds. Propriety made its demands, but certain kinds of freedom called out. There is the story of how Bennett, settled in Paris to write *The Old Wives' Tale*, offered to share his mistress with Maugham. She had two evenings a week free, and she liked writers, he said. The new bohemians, struggling to break free from the rigid proprieties of Victorian England, went to France where sexual release was more easily available. It was the city of *maisons de tolérance*, the place where certain celebrated courtesans were known as *les grandes horizontales*, where Degas returned obsessively to the brothels to draw his lean, accurate sketches of the women at leisure between customers.

A kind of freedom, freedom for men, and for some few women, those who could turn the conventions of the time to their own advantage. Once when I met Tarrington in Paris – we were both there doing research and met in a little café on the Quai des Grands Augustins, in the green light under the plane trees where he drank wine while I consoled myself with a café-crème – he spoke as if such a city still existed. Perhaps for him it did. He had left Madeleine behind in Canada, and he had two regular lovers, an American who was at the Sorbonne, and a young Frenchwoman he had picked up somewhere.

Madeleine was slow to suspect what he was up to. I found this out when I arrived back. She told me about it. That summer. She told me many things, some that I kept to myself for years after. That was the last summer that Tarrington lived among us here. Belle will remember the farewell parties as he prepared to go off into the great world. A last blow-out in their small bungalow, a corn roast on the beach. And the rest of it. The end of it all. Yes, Belle, we both remember.

I have seen you, Mr President, glancing at your watch, but you know my assignment. Fill the time. I am doing it. If you think my course as indirect as that of the river Meander, I will admit you are right, but it is surely no more roundabout than, let us say, the memoir by Clive Bell which is one of the sources of information about our artist. He wrote it many years after his first days in Paris, and he had reached the age when there are no straight lines in the tale of human experience.

Bell writes of Morrice's flute playing, beautiful until he grew short of breath. He remembers Morrice telling him that he played in the Hallé orchestra – which is almost certainly untrue, but then it is a story and as good as any story. I might tell you that I taught introductory physics at Harvard and met my wife there, a story no more unlikely. Both tales may be true. They ought to be. I must have met my wife somewhere, just as I lost her somewhere, and the scenes that are observed beyond the window, in the far distance, down the long vistas of perspective, are always unclear: tiny figures performing unidentified acts, the tiny dabs of black in the rich colour of a Paris evening. It was a conversation we had about just such things that led Tarrington to the writing of one of his first famous essays, 'The Triumph of the Background'. In those days the two of us were teaching sections of An Introduction to Civilization, the course which attempted to bring our students into a little intimacy with art, music, literature and philosophy through the ages. An Introduction to Glibness, the head of the French department called it.

I was speaking about the colour green. Morrice's Canadian paintings don't use it as one of their keynotes. There are lovely pink and purple shadows on the snow, and the light is usually the light of winter, grey and blue – though the original of his famous picture of the Quebec ferry, if examined carefully, has strokes of green in the ice, though they are almost impossible to see in small reproductions. There is so much we never see. Morrice chose not to see the greens of the green season in the Quebec countryside, because of its rapidity perhaps, the way the golden green of spring vanishes, is touched by darkness so soon and then gone, or because he was artistically blind to them. Part of the genius of any artist is his blindness. What he cannot see makes possible what he can. The long slow greens of rainy Paris hang in the air like the scent of smoke.

I've always enjoyed fine phrases. My record of publication is scant partly because ideas come to me in a likely phrase, a short paragraph, and the struggle to move from that to a coherently argued essay has been inordinately difficult. In youth, I was full of ambition, but the silences between the words conquered. In front of students, I was able to summarize and quote and add my own little insights. The repeated pattern from year to year, new faces in the same old seats, made it seem sufficiently commonplace that I didn't listen to my words. Here in front of you, it is something else, but I came knowing it was an emergency, inspired, perhaps, by the thought of that body lying dead on the tiles, and I will do my duty, after my fashion. I have often thought to write about Morrice, and I make regular trips to the Musée des Beaux Arts in Montreal to look at the collection of sketches on wood.

I can now count only two striped ties in the audience in front of me. Two ties in two seats of Madden Hall, where once there were three, and yet I was unaware of a departure. Perhaps my mind was on other things, as it should be, on history, art and badminton. Perhaps the man wearing the third striped tie did not in fact leave but slipped it quickly off. It might even be one of those ties that clips onto the collar, though I haven't seen one of those for years, but with such a tie, it would be the work of a second to remove it. In a moment of self-consciousness or cunning after I was bold enough to mention the presence of these three men with the strip of stripes that would identify them to each other. Now one has abandoned his team, his tie hidden in his pocket. Take that, cravat. Or perhaps he only got bored and angry and slipped out when I was staring up to the ceiling for energy and inspiration.

Bored and angry: Tarrington's rage, *La Furia di Tarrington*, that remarkable piece of baroque nonsense for the keyboard.

Biography, you will have noticed in your past reading, and I'm certain you are one of those who has, Mr President, is often an invitation to bad writing, what is thought to evoke the times and places of the past, usually with the direst consequences.

You know the sort of thing. *In old Quebec Morrice would see the happy peasants tramping in from the countryside with their baskets of fresh farm produce, charming and colourful personages in brightest homespun. Then he came to Paris, the streets of the yellow fiacres, with his most magic flute, his passion for the pigments, and his great and high purpose.* An attempt to make the *mélange* of fact and opinion and rumour that is the source of biography into a story, usually the imitation of tawdry fictions already existing, whereas life, as we all know, is not a story at all. It is the music of no mind.

The shuttlecock summer. Back and forth. You will excuse my pun. Those of you who play badminton, will know the excitement of the slow rise and soft fall of the shuttlecock. It has about it a rare beauty, lovelier than the meaningless bouncing of balls in tennis and squash. It is a quiet game, only the sudden soft exhalations of breath as the player runs into position and lifts the bird high over the court or niftily slices it into the corner by the net. As I have explained, my wife Anne and I could usually defeat Denman and Madeleine. We were never so close as with rackets in our hands, had the unspoken ability to share the court even in the quickest passages of the game, whereas Madeleine's long elegant legs were, in the stress of competition, a little ungainly, and her husband tried to play the whole game himself, pushing her out of the way now and then to get at the bird, preventing her from making shots that she could have returned if left to herself. After every loss, we were treated to *La Furia di Tarrington*, and one sometimes wondered what Madeleine had to endure once he got her home. Anne, though she had shorter legs, pink and soft-thighed, breasts that slithered and bounced, was very quick on her feet and had an intuitive sense of where the opponent would move next so that the shuttlecock dropped just where the enemy used to be. It was my duty to drive Denman to the back of the court with long lobs and smashes while Anne finished the point with finesse.

After the game, we would recover our baby daughter from the sitter, and we might go to their house, or sometimes Denman and Madeleine would come round for an Ovaltine against the cold winter night. In the hour we spent together, as Denman and I bragged about the clever things we had said in lectures and set out our plans for the books we were to

write, *La Furia di Tarrington* would, I hoped, calm itself so
that Madeleine would have less to endure when they got
home.

To move on, move on. I have a story about Picasso, which
I recall from Clive Bell's book of memories. I have said that
one of Bell's subjects was J. W. Morrice, whose friend he
became on his first trip to Paris. Like all personal accounts of
the painter, it is affectionate and favourable. He seems to
have maintained his charm even when far gone in drink, an
unusual enough characteristic, as we all know, who have been
among the bores and vulgarians of late-night gatherings. In a
journal, Arnold Bennett remarked of Morrice that he had the
joy of life in a high degree, and he gave this characteristic, the
delight in every detail of existence observed, to the character
he based on his friend. Clive Bell claimed that it was from
Morrice that he learned to enjoy Paris. That faculty of
enjoyment was surely linked to the speed and small size of his
oil sketches.

But Picasso. Picasso and the bath: in a discussion of
miracles, the great Pablo said that he thought it a miracle
that he didn't melt in his morning bath. This was during the
days of his first marriage and rich respectability, and someone
who heard him remarked that a few years before, one
wouldn't have believed he knew what a bath was for.

In those days, in France, it was possible to have a bath
sent in. A team of men carried in the tub and hot water and
disposed of it when you were done. Bell knew a man who
knew an actress who had one sent in to her top floor flat once
a week. Women bathing, it has been a subject from Degas and
Bonnard to the TV commercial. The peeper's delight. The long
slender body in subtle tones of iridescent milky white, with
touches of mauve and perhaps a little hint of green reflected
from the leaves outside the window. She is bent to dry herself
with the blue towel, and that too casts a little reflection on the
hospitable skin. Outside the open window, a chirping of

23

sparrows and the sound of a car driving by. Didn't know whose car, wondered.

I am not aware that our man Morrice ever painted a woman bathing. There are a few finely done nudes, and one astonishing portrait, now in the possession of the National Gallery in Ottawa, which is as sexual as any nude, though in fact only the head and bare shoulders of the model are seen, as she looks toward us from the top right corner of the painting, while most of the canvas is the remarkably delicate and sensual painting of the bedsheets. Though the model is unidentified, the name Jane is painted into the texture in large pale letters, and the small canvas evokes the greatest possible intimacy. The woman naked beneath the covers. The commonplace miracle.

Tarrington lying naked on the tiles after his last ecstasy.

This is not easy to believe, and I am myself astonished, but now suddenly I see only one striped tie among you. Is this a game? My eyes, at least with the aid of these spectacles, are accurate enough, and I know what I see. Three striped appendages. Then only one. Certainly I have noticed one or two people departing from the dim back corner, but the striped ties were, each one of them, buried among you, well forward in the light.

Wake up, Frank Puncheon. I see you there with your eyes closed. I know, as an astronomer emeritus you are compelled to be up half the night staring at stars, but it's only proper to pinch yourself and pay attention. In front of you, the three short-haired young female lecturers are doing me the courtesy of smiling and nodding even though I am a Dead White Male. You can do as much. You know badminton yourself. We used to play from time to time. I remember a particularly vicious slashing game just after we both had proposals for conference papers turned down. Tarrington, then creeping toward fame, was on my committee, though I fail to remember who was on yours.

One of the errors in your introduction, Mr President, was
in the matter of my involvement with the local naturalists'
society. I was not merely one of those involved in bringing
the annual bird count to the district, I was in fact the first of
those to bring the bird count to this part of the country, and
my birding columns were not merely published in the local
press but were syndicated throughout eastern Canada and
certain of the New England States. Credit where credit is
due. Though I never became a celebrity, I played my part in
life. An attendant lord? One would hope not just that. You
will be able to place the quotation, Mr President, from your
memories of Introductory Civilization. You were, of course,
in Tarrington's section, and I remember he said you were not
much inclined to work but didn't need to as you would
inherit a thriving chain of stores. It has been observed often
enough that you have been good about passing on some of
your profits to this institution and bringing your moneyed
friends into the fold. Thus the Jakeson lectures, funded by
your in-laws, Jakeson and Jakeson. So, as I acknowledge
your good works, you will allow me the cavils of an old
scholar.

Now in all this, we have forgotten someone. We have
forgotten that man in a small office in Ottawa, an upstairs
office on Sparks Street. It was a street in those days, a dim
street of heavy buildings, though it is now a pedestrian mall
where buskers come out to amuse the tourists who are in
town to see the Parliament Buildings all sharp and Gothic on
their hill above the wide river. I often take an early morning
bus from Montreal to Ottawa and go to the National Gallery
to see the Morrices, some other things by his friend Cullen,
and a few other favourites. There is a charming painting by a
certain W. Blair Bruce, an artist contemporary with Morrice
and Cullen. It's called *Joy of the Nereids* and is a bubbling
waterfall of nudes, a big painting, perhaps eight feet square,
and in splendidly garish colours. It brings a smile to my face

when all else fails. I recommend it. A sovereign cure for melancholy, and a splendid spread of naked belles.

Belles with an 'e'. An old-fashioned term, but appropriate enough to the period. Belle as in Annabelle, and you were, weren't you? *Nous n'irons plus au bois.* The man in the office, we are forgetting him again. He thinks, sometimes, that he was born to be forgotten. A few years before, he was a manager for a large firm selling office supplies, but the business failed in the Depression, and he was thrown on the street. For a short while he was reduced to selling insurance, but a friend who felt sorry for him told the Canadian Committee that he was the perfect man to manage their office. Until then he had thought very little about his patriotic duties, and early in life had considered moving to Chicago, but he was willing enough to become a patriot if there was a job in it. His children are beginning to be grown, and in fact his son, a feckless boy who quit school last year and delivers groceries on his bicycle, spending his pocket money on smokes, will come of age just in time to join the army for the war which is now imminent. He will die on the beach at Dieppe, and his father will wonder forever afterward if they might have been friends some day. Our man keeps very busy during the war, for the Canadian Committee takes on a number of contributions to the war effort, some of them in collaboration with the YMCA, and at the end of the war he will find a job running the Ottawa branch of the Y, and he will stay there until retirement. He has two daughters, but we will not enquire as to what destiny intends for them.

Earlier in my lecture, when I mentioned the inaccurate rumour of Morrice's death, I failed to mention the odd fact that this is an echo of a book, Arnold Bennett's *Buried Alive*, a book in which the character of the hero, Priam Farll, is derived in some small ways from Morrice. In that story, an artist still alive is believed to be dead. It is all a shade farcical. The incorrect reports about Morrice's death were spread partly because of his vanishing acts. Especially later in life, his friends often had no idea where he was. He would pack up and go at the slightest provocation. Léa Cadoret, his mistress, was accustomed to receiving a card mailed from a railway station announcing that he was off to Cuba or Morocco or Canada. He must have known that his health was failing near the end, for he bought her a house in the south of France. Not many years later he died in Tunis, alone.

We prefer, of course, to remember him in Paris, in his chair at a café, his paints in a little box in his pocket, to be taken out for one of those sudden tiny oils, the work punctuated by absinthe or whisky. Sometimes, when he needed a figure in one of the sketches, just there, a punctuation, he would send Léa over to stand in the right spot, and she obliged. She was clearly devoted to this curious lovable man, and he treated her well in his absent-minded, occasional, evanescent way. She had first come to him as a model, and it was easy enough to stand on the cobbled street, the kiosk in the background, the evening life of Paris going on around them, sudden dabs of black in the picture. A love story of a sort. There are so many. I called Morrice the prince of all the greens, but he was also king of the blacks. Never such speed and suddenness as the picture of figures and pigeons in the Piazza San Marco. Everything is there and flying. Black figures, black feathers, in one of the golden cities.

Once such things were in private collections, hidden on the walls of great houses and high apartments, and some are even yet, but more and more, they are in museums. If you own an important painting, you are caught between the thieves and the company that insures you against their depredations. Maugham, in his later days, growing anxious and irritable as old men do, was at last so terrified that his paintings might be stolen that he sold them all, even those he had given to his daughter. Ashes, ashes, we all fall down. Denman Tarrington fell down in that small bathroom. It might have been the subject of one last essay. 'Dying in the Steam: A Mist that Never Rises.'

The café where we met: I had walked along the Seine on my way and I had puzzled over his appetites and the ease with which he satisfied them. That summer, his first essay had appeared in *Partisan Review*, and he had been invited to New York to meet Philip Rahv. At least half of that essay was derived from conversation between the two of us, and I no longer knew which ideas were mine, but some of them were. He took them without so much as a by-your-leave, as he would always take what he wanted. If I had written the essay, it would have been more coherent and less successful. I looked down at a barge passing along the Seine, laundry hung across the deck behind the cabin, and I half imagined the life lived on the boat, a boat just like one of those passing by the Quai des Grands Augustins in the Morrice paintings I loved even then, though I had seen fewer of them.

As I walked toward the café, I saw Tarrington seated at one of the tables, making notes in a small book. When he saw me, he put it away. At the end of the summer, he would be leaving us for a more prestigious university, and there would be no more badminton games. No more Ovaltine on wintry nights, no more feeling sorry for Madeleine. Much more than that to be lost, though I couldn't know it then. As we met in Paris, Madeleine was back in their little house organizing the move, beautiful, awkward, unhappy. Anne was away, visiting her aunt, but I expected to find her at home when I got off the plane a few days later, though when I got there the house was empty; she had extended her visit. I sat down at the table with Tarrington and ordered, and it was only a few minutes before he was telling me about the pubic bouquet – both senses – of his American girl, and the cleverness of the French one. It was a mystery to me then and is now how Tarrington gained the belief that everyone loved him, and that he was excused in advance for all the wanton acts he might care to commit, that women would adore him in spite of his faithlessness, that the world would open its doors at his approach, that his lies would become truth once they were spoken, or if not become truth be found necessary and right in some other way. The blood that was shed was never his responsibility. Could I, one day, learn to shed blood?

I told you about the conversation I overheard about tattoos. One of the young women reported to the other that her boyfriend wanted her to put roses on her butt, as she phrased it. Tarrington would have made that sort of demand, and possibly some woman would have acceded, would have been willing to be branded for him. The secrecy of secret marks, a part of intimacy. Perhaps after the lecture, the clever young women academics in the second row will discuss this with me, and I can pass on their wisdom in the next lecture.

Astonishing. The last striped tie is gone. I wonder if their departures are carefully timed, and with an obscure significance that I have been unable to work out. There are those who believe that everything in the world is significant, that a pattern exists, whether or not we can perceive it. My wife Anne was known to read the horoscopes. She suspected that forces were moving outside the bounds of our awareness. As if the three men in striped ties might now be gathered somewhere in the dark corner of the physics lab, listening to the humming of the cyclotron and comparing notes on my lecture, to make sure that between the three of them they have an accurate record of what I said.

Anne had a secret mark on her lower back. Sometimes I would stare at it, and try to describe it to her. It is like an Egyptian hieroglyph of a bird, I would say. It is like a tarragon leaf. It is like a like a dark and slender insect, perfectly still, waiting for its prey. It is the precise shape of your immortal soul. She flushed easily, blood mantling her skin. When we played badminton, her face grew pink and damp, and she had a way of pushing her hair back with her left hand.

That is what I recall. Once I thought of writing a work of fiction about the early years here. A question, of course, as to how a work of fiction can be about a real time and place. The reading of literary biography is unsettling in the way it shows us how writers mix experience, gossip and lies and call the whole gallimaufry a novel. Arnold Bennett's *Buried Alive*, as I have said, tells a long and unlikely story about an artist who is alive though believed dead. A note on influences: the painter's wife in that book strikes me as quite possibly the source for Joyce Cary's Sara Monday. Books are made from other books, as a critic observes. And paintings from other paintings. Lectures from other lectures. Of course both Bennett and Cary are out of style, and no one is likely to care how one book was made out of another book, one wife out of another wife. Late on in Bennett's novel, when his hero has gone back to painting, Bennett attributes to him a painting which is exactly an oil done by his friend J. W. Morrice – though he says it is a painting of London, when in fact it is Paris. The painting is now in Ottawa in the National Gallery. On the very next page, whether as a joke or an apology, Bennett mentions Morrice, side by side with his contemporary Bonnard. This is not imagination so much as a set of gossipy games. Everything is connected, but not by the force of the stars.

My copy of this Bennett novel, now long out of print, came from a second-hand bookstore like so many of my books. I have fewer now, of course, having left many of them with your library when I moved to Montreal. I hope the library has not tossed them all out. *Library Discard. Library Discard.* I didn't check when I was there, though I did pick up a copy of the recent library newsletter with its story about the early manuscripts given to the institution last summer by Denman Tarrington, probably when he was asked to inaugurate the

Jakeson lectures. I asked to see them, but they are not yet catalogued, and so are inaccessible. I don't know how much of a saver he was, our DT – I used to refer to him as Professor Delirium Tremens – but if he was a saver of everything that touched his important life, as I suspect he was, there are letters of mine in the hoard. Letters from long ago, threats and explanations. Perhaps he never opened them.

Arnold Bennett, Somerset Maugham, Clive Bell, the three literary blokes who moved through the bohemian world of Paris and met the charming, brilliant, alcoholic Canadian painter, and then of course went on to other lives. Maugham became, among other things, a spy, married in odd circumstances and later complained to Glenway Westcott that his wife's physical demands were intolerable, inexcusable. The myth of nymphomania, a word that was current in my youth, though I think it is now gone out of common usage. Later on, intemperate desire was advertised as both common and exemplary. Witness Denman Tarrington's fame. Then came disease and a return to prudence.

More often than uncontrollable female appetite, a joint madness, nymph and nympholept in a state of demoniac possession for reasons beyond our power to express. The one tireless, the other insatiable. Nothing to do with love, but many have known what it was like, a woman possessed and needing to be possessed endlessly, for beyond was a vacuum, merest nothingness. Maugham's wife knew she could not have him, a cold man and a homosexual, so she would have his services, would insist on being filled. That he was horrified was only partly his misogyny. It was a terror of what lay beyond, the emptiness that could not be filled. Yes, it was like that.

I am stopping too frequently now for these sips of water. My throat grows dry, and my legs are aching from the time spent here at this lectern. I am coming toward the end of my allotted time. The three striped ties have vanished, and that is a signal. It is regrettable, perhaps, that the slides were left in that taxi, for those of you who haven't seen Morrice's paintings will be left with only my verbal evocations of them. There are books available in your library. I checked, when I was not listening to an essay on tattoos, and those of you who are interested may go there and see the only barely adequate reproductions. Or you may also get yourselves to the collections in Montreal and Ottawa. I recommend it.

I was a young man when I first became aware of some of those paintings. I was a young man. That in itself is a surprising thing, for I am now as you observe me, but once I was lean and quick on my feet, racing backward and forward on the badminton court, wrist and arm tireless, sweating only a little from the exertion as I dodged about, Anne's figure, sturdy and pink, as quick as my own. On the other side of the net, Denman Tarrington's sharp-featured, bearded face – I wonder how often the beard smelled of a recent student – Madeleine's tall, somehow helpless body reaching out, and sometimes, with her long reach, she would catch one of our shots, against all likelihood of its being caught, and lift it over the net, and I was aware of a kind of shudder of relief going through her body. Outside, always, the snow.

Apparently Morrice's winter scenes were mostly painted in his studio in Paris from pencil sketches and oil *pochades* done on the spot. His back turned to the window over the Seine, he studied the Canadian landscape in his mind and gradually, each morning adding a few more strokes, he made it real on canvas.

I will keep you from the important duties of your lives only a moment more. Indulge me just a little. You remember our friend in Ottawa, working for the Canadian Committee, filling out order forms for copies of the biography of J. W. Morrice, though in fact he has never seen the painter's work but has read a review of the book and believes that it is important, and it is among those he will see distributed to the army, navy and air force, a testimony to the importance of the country they serve. Then as he sits at his table in the small office, doing the work for which he is paid very little – though it is better than the hopeless idleness that came before it – he thinks of his wife, at home, waiting for him in the dim November afternoon, and he tries to imagine her as she was before he met her, tries to reach that ghost of the future, and is aware that he cannot.

Tomorrow afternoon, I will offer the second lecture in the series. I trust you will all be here once again.

Two

It was kind of you to offer that little reception for me after yesterday's lecture, even though a number of those invited took flight after five minutes, and I did overhear one or two remarks that were characterized more by irony than comprehension. *We know what he means by no mind, don't we?* That sort of thing, tossed off by those who have learned all too well that worst academic habit, sly condescension. Even as an undergraduate, I was aware that a certain kind of thing that passed for wit was the anxious cruelty of the uncertain.

Your president, who has bravely come back for my second performance, was generous in the face of my cavilling at his introduction and its inaccuracies. Little enough time for research, as he observed. We were both forced to speak on little notice. I had three days to prepare, he little more than three hours, he told me. So we have agreed that we both did our best in the circumstances. I do confess that it was dim-witted of me to lose the box of slides, though I had only a limited number prepared which were appropriate to my subjects. I hope they turn up. Most were slides I had used in my undergraduate lectures at this very institution.

One of the brisk and skull-shaven young women in row two – and I notice you have all come back, very good of you – said that she felt wholly unable to predict what I would choose to talk about in my second lecture but there you are, back for more. I could have claimed to have no idea myself of what I would say next, but you will see that there is a pad of notes and sketches here, places to start, *obiter dicta* that may be offered and glossed. Here, for example is a note that says: *The homogeneity of time, the condition of waiting.* I'm not sure we'll get to that one. I'm certain that when I scratched it down, I had something in mind. Is time homogeneous? Perhaps some physicist in the audience will let me know.

Our last lecture got us to Paris, and another of the quotations in front of me is about Paris, written by Walter Benjamin, about the city's mirrors, the immaterial element of the city, he calls them, and you will recall how often in a small café or restaurant you look up from the table, and a mirror will show you those who stand by the bar, and behind them, the buildings on the street outside. You may be familiar with the photographs of Brassai, how we catch the sense of ongoing life in the mirrors of the bars where he took pictures, two lovers, his face in one mirror, hers in another at right angles to the first. Love is this and this, but also this and this, and the mirror holds it without comment.

After the reception yesterday, I walked back to my room in a pleasant motel just down the road, and as soon as I was inside, one of the mirrors caught me and showed me myself. As I looked, I thought about that old trick of exposition, found in bad fiction, where the main character looks in the mirror and the author is able to describe the long pale face, the white hair combed straight across, the pattern of wrinkles beside the eyes, the thin mouth that might be about to smile. A face that a woman, in the grip of whatever madness, once called beautiful. You know the sort of thing. The mirror gives us an author's-eye-view of ourselves. When I walked into the bathroom, there was yet another, larger mirror, as there was in that hotel room in New York where Denman Tarrington could admire his naked body before stepping into the shower.

No one who wasn't a thoroughgoing narcissist could have lived his life. Each morning, he stood there, a little heavier, the face giving the impression of solid slabs of flesh with slight declivities where the slabs met, the long arms hanging from the sturdy body, a little ape-like perhaps, but effective for seizing the ripe fruit of life. Once he had those arms round a woman's body, there was no escape. Still pretty well hung, he would think to himself, as he observed the thing in repose.

I reflected as I stood in the bathroom of that motel, that if he had survived to come here and speak, he would have looked in the same mirror, stood where I was now standing. The two of us were there for a moment, side by side, as if washing up after a brisk hour on the badminton court. Then I turned my back, sent him once again to the underworld.

We are accustomed to mirrors by now, but once they were rare and expensive. The first mirrors were polished metal discs, hand mirrors that showed only the face. Before those metal discs, men and women had only the surface of the still pool, but that was enough for Narcissus. Fell in love with himself and that was the end of him. Perhaps the mirror changed history. Brunelleschi began his studies of perspective by drawing what he saw in a mirror, and it was only in twentieth-century art that his mirror was shattered.

For now I see through a glass, darkly, Paul says, in a passage we all know, and I suppose the reference is to an early mirror of poor quality, glass of limited transparency, full of flaws, backed unevenly with silver, but now the mirrors are perfect and the flaws are in the face observed.

I was in the middle of these reflections last night when the telephone rang, and I picked it up, for once unthinking, wondering if perhaps it was someone who had been assigned to take me out for dinner at the Boat Shed, always my favourite restaurant, but the instant I lifted the phone, I could hear the silence, and I said Hello, and Hello and Hello, and there was nothing, and I hung up. Beyond the motel window it was snowing. The calls had stopped, or so I believed. One or two after I moved to Montreal. Now another. Looking into the audience I search among your faces for the half-forgotten face, come here to watch me, to listen and then late at night to make a call, but there is nothing to be found. Are you there? No.

When the phone rang again, later on, I found it hard to

39

answer, but I did and it was my daughter Sylvia calling from Victoria to ask how the lecture had gone. Now that we are back in touch, she tries to be good to me. I described the lecture to her, but of course she thought I was joking. Perhaps I was.

I see you, Belle, slipping in the back door. Hello. A little late. Well, I was afraid you had abandoned me. Tomorrow after the last lecture we must get together and bring back old times over dinner. I have been speaking, while you were struggling here through the snow, of the mirrors of Paris, the mind of the city which watches, unmoved, the little adventures of life. The mirrors on the walls of the brothel where the act is seen and then the empty room is unseen. As if the rooms might expect our coming, that room in the motel anticipating my return, my apartment in Montreal full of familiar shapes and smells although I am not there. The mirrors on the brothel wall offer a doubling or, with facing mirrors, a tripling and then a projection of the act to infinity, a hint that we can know the unknowable. He knew her and she was with child, as the Bible would have it, but of course he knew nothing. He stirred the nerves.

One of my favourite of Brassaï's photos is of two women in a bar, the bartender seen in the mirror at an odd angle, and for me, it evokes Manet's great painting of the bar of the Folies-Bergère, a painting which is now in the Courtauld Institute. One can read essays about Manet's painting, and what we can or can't see in the mirror behind the lovely-looking young woman who is tending bar. The reason he is a great painter is that the questions he asks are not the same as the questions he answers. The portrait of the barmaid was the first in which he used a mirror, though Ingres and Degas had used the device earlier. Here the observer is struck by the oddity of the reflection which appears to be an angled view though seen in a straight mirror. You will all have seen prints of the painting, and I will not tell you what you already know, except to say that if he had used the mirror in a mechanical way, what we would see is the artist at his easel, but in this case the painter has disappeared, and his absence is as powerful as the unspeaking voice at the other end of my phone call.

I will come back to a painting where the artist is seen in the mirror. Perhaps you can guess what I'm referring to. We are all, of course, thrown back on memory by my absent-minded loss of the slides, and while some have a capacious and accurate visual memory – I have tried to train my own – others have only a few vague impressions, and those who have never seen copies of the pictures I refer to can only take my word for what is there. As easy as to imagine Tarrington's sturdy body lying dead in the steam. As easy as to imagine Madeleine standing beside me on the shore in the dark as the soft lap of the rising tide moved over our bare feet. As easy … well, you take my point.

Until I came to this university as a young man, recently married and a father, I had never lived near salt water. I was raised among long streets and flat country, bicycle rides and baseball, slow dusty summer evenings. From the window of the house we rented when we came here, a house we purchased two years later, you could see a narrow stretch of water some distance off over the marshes. It is still there, that big frame house. Some of you will know it. It was too big for the three of us, but when we arrived, it was for rent, and Anne wanted it. When we first examined it, she stared out the window at the water, which was blue that day, reflecting a blue sky, and the marsh the drying green of late summer, and when she turned from the window, I could read the expression on her face and see that she wanted to live here. I was not always able to read that face.

Difficult to read the face of Manet's woman, the one behind the bar, in front of the long, deceptive mirror. As a model he used, not a professional, but a woman who actually

41

worked at that bar, though who is to say why? He had a complicated way of confronting reality, not quite one thing or the other. If you study the original, you will find that the painting moves in receding levels. The effect is lost in reproductions. Manet asked, as I have said, one question and answered a different one. The music of no mind.

One of the women who came to last night's reception enquired if, given my title, I would be making reference to the history of music in these lectures, and I explained that although I mentioned music in the title, I would not. I understand the sound of music only when it is overheard, in fragments, perhaps from another room or from a passing car. That is music, the momentary haunting of the air by fascinating sounds, but the continuous scratching of fiddles is meaningless. Words too are best when overheard. Behind my back, just at that moment, as I was discussing music, a voice was saying, *She was never seen again.* My ears are not what they once were, all the senses growing dull, but I did hear that, a sentence summing up a life. She was never seen again.

The window of our house looked over the salt marsh toward that tongue of sea, and I kept binoculars hung close by so that I could watch the birds that appeared there. Birds to come in my third lecture. Below the window was the lawn where Anne and I would sometimes play a sort of badminton with no net. Yes, I know what Robert Frost said about free verse, though I'm not sure of its application to marital badminton. Our daughter Sylvia was only a little thing in those days, and while she was a charming child, she was a child, and Anne was alone with her for long hours while I prepared classes and marked assignments and attempted to finish my doctoral thesis. Never did. Tarrington, of course, had completed his before arriving, a year after we came here. Years later he referred to my difficulties in another of his early essays, 'Night Baseball: Rules of the Academic Game'.

Young, we all were, and recently married. Wedding

photographs on the bedroom dresser. The long article on the symbolism of wedding photographs is one of the pieces of writing I did finish, as your president told you when he introduced me yesterday. Got that one right, rushed as you were, Mr President.

In fact that essay was meant to be the start of a book. I had in mind a companion piece about the most famous of all wedding portraits, the van Eyck oil usually called the Arnolfini Wedding, which always made me think of my own wedding photograph. If you look in the indexes, you will find a long list of articles on van Eyck's picture, but for our purposes, the matter at issue is one small section in the upper half. The convex mirror. A favourite device in the Flemish artists of the period, Campin (or whoever it was painted what is attributed to him), Petrus Christus, Memling, Quentin Matsys, they all show their skill by rendering the glossy surface of the mirror and the odd corner of reality it catches. Of course we know little about those old Flemish masters, and among scholars there is a rage to name artists who might better be left anonymous so that we are invigorated by our ignorance, rather than stifled by what we believe we know.

Was she pregnant? A great belly brought into being by that long-faced expressionless man beside her. It's easily enough done, or was in the days before the pill. I gather, of course, that we are now in the days after the pill. Dangers to health of one sort or another. My friends in the second row will enlighten me later on. If I were as prolific as the lamented Tarrington, I would write an essay on the shaved head and new standards of female beauty. Yes, my dear, I have a shrewd suspicion that you are differently inclined, but the shape of your scalp is very appealing, and though not a professional lecher like DT, I have never been able to keep my eyes off certain women.

And that is how my wife became my wife, quite against

her better judgement. She didn't wish to marry me, but she did.

The convex mirror in the wedding portrait: look closely, though of course you can't because I-the-dolt lost the slides, but look closely at your memory, walk up close to it in a certain room in that building on Trafalgar Square, while outside, your friend who hates art is waiting impatiently to go for a cream tea, and what you see in that reflecting fish eye is the backs of the happy couple and two other more distant figures, behind the plane of the painting, invisible except in the mirror, and one of them is the artist himself. *Johannes de Eyck fuit hic.* Kilroy was here, that ubiquitous phrase from the days after the Second War, originally a soldier's joke perhaps. The painting is the world's fanciest marriage certificate, some would tell us, but of course it is not evidence as a photograph might be, for it would have taken months to paint, and the details are all thought to be symbolic – imagine a dog as the symbol of sexual fidelity all you who have found one humping your knee – but like the tourist's photograph of himself standing in front of the Pietà, the painting is offered as proof that the event took place, all of this in the face of the multiplicity and evanescence of what occurs. Bang, zip, gone. We hear a voice singing as we walk away down the street. The semen spurts and nine times out of ten the whole thing is lost in the next thing to happen. Now and then, the belly swells.

Giovanna Cenami might not have been pregnant. It may be the fashion of the dress, the long train that she holds against her front. The orange on the table symbol of something. The fruit of marriage. The vegetable of adultery – that is a whimsical, if private reference to the occasion when a woman handed me a carrot whittled into the shape of an erect penis. Never offer to help in the kitchen.

The other convex mirrors in paintings of the period are more indirect in their reference. The primary reason for their use in the painting was, I imagine, to show off the painter's skill, like all those empty wineglasses, brass vessels, the sort of gear that allowed the exploitation of illusion. Look what I can do in showing the gleaming surface of the world. Look how I can paint a mirror.

Max Beerbohm possessed a convex mirror. His father bought it at the Paris International Exhibition of 1867, and it was in the young Max's nursery, then stayed with him all his life. There is always a fascination with such things, the way they reach out and bring the whole room to a focus in the watcher's eye. It was suggested that Beerbohm intended to write an autobiographical novel about that mirror, but it never happened. The idea is an intriguing one but misses the point of course. The mirror reflects everything and sees nothing. It has no mind. *We know what he means by no mind, don't we?* I will remember that wisecrack.

Beerbohm's convex mirror showing the curve of life, the man in old age, dry and astute. One of the other essays I once planned was to be about artists in their last days. Matisse still drawing when he couldn't rise from bed. Saying he wasn't sick, he was injured, and calling himself *un grand mutilé.* Monet's colours getting brighter as his vision went until he was making neon scribbles of the Japanese bridge. In my first lecture, I told you a story about Maugham's senile rage. Perhaps I am ready to write that essay now.

Artists growing older, and I am at the age when, inevitably, one looks back. I still have a copy of the wedding photo that sat on the dresser of our rented house, and when I look at it, I think that we were young and knew nothing – which means, of course, we knew the insistent truths of eager selfishness and animal appetite. I had a smuggled copy of *Lady Chatterley's Lover* – it was legal a few years afterward – and we read it aloud to each other with the predictable effect. We slapped the little feathered shuttlecock across the lawn at each other in the summer evening while a hawk hunted over the marsh and our daughter slept in her bedroom upstairs, and as the sun went down, it flashed in my eyes until I couldn't see to play the game.

When we decided to buy that house, I did some research on its history. The documentary material I came up with is in the archives of the local historical society, and Janice Baglioni will make it available to you if you are interested. The builder was William Smithson, who is recorded to have built a number of houses here in the period from 1890 to 1905. He had an interest in Doggett's mill, and the wood for the houses was milled there. He seems to have worked from a pattern book he got hold of somewhere in New England, and the houses often look as if they belong in Massachusetts or Connecticut. Isabel Smithson, his daughter, was still alive when I was doing my research, and though she had a reputation for being strange, perhaps even mad, she knew things, and if you had the patience, information could be obtained. I spent some hours sitting at her kitchen table with a cold cup of tea, running my fingers over the checked oilcloth while I waited for her to remember, or perhaps only to agree to tell me what she remembered. She lived, as we say, in another world, and talking to her, you went back in time into the previous century. When I told Denman Tarrington about her, he was convinced that she had been sexually misused by her father in the years when the two of them lived alone together, and that was why she could not get past the year 1900, but I was not convinced. Another of Tarrington's vulgarities. Not everything can be explained by what's between the legs, I said to him, and he laughed, but I am here and laughing last.

The wood was hauled from the mill by a horse and wagon, and as the men unloaded it, Smithson would scribble patterns in the dirt, imagining the shapes that were to be built, and then he would give orders to the other carpenter who worked with him and to the apprentices, and they would set the wood on sawhorses and begin to cut the framing members. Behind the hole in the ground where the foundation was to be built, the red-winged blackbirds were loud at the edge of the marsh. I can't explain why, but I always thought of that big frame place as the Summer House, even when January blizzards were swirling past the windows. It held summer in its memory, and I could never bear to leave it until I retired and decided to go away altogether. Peaceful out there by the salt marshes, in the empty house, and it was not easy to grow used to the noise of life, all the radios and television sets and babbling newspapers and signals arriving from all over the planet. The gibbering of the eternal spaces frightens me, to abuse a familiar quotation. You will allow me my little games.

Petrus Christus, he of the odd name, is the next on our list. Peter Christ. Another craftsman going carefully about his work. Scholars battle about dates and influences, though the facts are few and all awash in suppositions. The painting we're concerned with is dated, so we can be certain that it was done fifteen years after the van Eyck wedding picture, and can perhaps assume that he got the idea of using a convex mirror from van Eyck's work, though there is no proof he ever saw it. Perhaps he received a suggestion from a gossipy visitor.

The subject of our painting is another couple, lovers, perhaps about to be married since they are visiting the jeweller, to get a ring we may suppose, though in this case the jeweller has a halo, picked out in delicate pale lines about his head as he weighs up a bit of gold on a balance in his hand and looks upward. That makes him St Eligius, the patron saint of gold and silversmiths. Not easy to tell whether he is looking beyond the lovers to some heavenly wisdom or whether the painter's draftsmanship was faulty. Certainly, as I recall the painting, the eyes of the lovers are fixed on the gold.

The climax of courtship, the moment when the ring is chosen: not perhaps a scene to be found in every wedding album today, but interesting enough, and in this case its

47

importance is guaranteed by the sainthood of our jeweller. A marriage made in heaven and at the bank, just as it should be, and documented by an expensive painting done by one of the best in Bruges.

Our point here is the mirror, and when the young couple saw the image, one wonders that they didn't send the painting back, for what is reflected there, by the magic of optics and the curvature of the device, is a street scene somewhere outside the jeweller's shop, quite possibly a cheat on the optical inevitabilities since it's not clear whether we are looking through a door or a window – a large doorway perhaps – in order to see the houses across the way. In front of those houses are two other figures, tiny commentators visible only in the upper body, the one, who seems to hold a large bird, perhaps a bird of prey, turned to the other with the sly vile expression of a malicious gossip. *He's only marrying her for the money, you know. That baker's girl in the square is with child and he's the one who set the loaf to rising. I've heard the things he says about her, what he will do with her money, and how he will keep her silent and obedient. She's got a bad one in him.* Perhaps I misread the painting, and if we had the slide, you might form your own opinion, but as it is, you are left with mine. Perhaps some of you know the painting. It is in the Met in New York and not out of reach. I looked at it on a recent visit.

The irony of van Eyck is gentle, a whimsical joke by which he places himself in the painting and shows himself as witness to the important ceremony, which, even if the bride is up the stump, is treated in a serious way. He loved painting the texture of the clothes, of course, and the symbolism may be taken as a pedestrian labelling, but still the technique is perfect, and the event is placed in time as a crystal wineglass might be placed on velvet.

Mr Christ, however, had none of this delicacy. No doubt he was paid a goodly sum to show the two lovers just when they

48

should be seen, as good Protestants, guaranteeing the union with an investment in gold, but I have always wondered what he told the purchasers of the painting they were seeing in the mirror. Maybe it was other members of the family. The two mothers-in-law, the price of the painting adjusted upward for each extra figure included. They have the look of the conventional mother-in-law, snide and disapproving.

Myself, I never had a mother-in-law, for Anne had been orphaned – an accident, then a heart attack, the two perhaps related – before I met her. She had a kindly aunt who came to the wedding and smiled, though she can't have been entirely pleased with the situation. It had not been easy to convince Anne to give in to necessity and accept me, but I insisted. I wanted her quietness, her lovely skin. She never put her reservations in words. Perhaps the figure in our convex mirror was Anne's other face, as sly and disapproving as those two gossips.

We could, while on the subject of mirrors, take a step to one side and lob the bird, look, there it goes, a little white object against the summer sky, into the territory of literature. There's the Lady of Shallott, virgin evader, and some nice lines of Auden's about Ferdinand and Miranda in his poems from *The Tempest*. *'My dear one is mine as mirrors are lonely.'* Very pretty, though I'm not sure I could explain what it means. Virginity again, that white thing that we no longer understand. A strange obsession to make virginity sacred. Prudence on the subject, well yes, whether at the level of health, self-respect or commerce, none of them a romantic or holy matter, we can be sure, and I wouldn't knock anyone's choice of prudence even if it means keeping your legs crossed for a long time, but the sacredness of the hymen is another matter altogether. I suppose Freud got it right. Sex had become undervalued in the Roman empire and the pendulum swung the other way. Asceticism made it a Big Thing. The metaphors are having their way with me.

That was another of the essays that Tarrington stole from our conversations; 'The Virgin's Breast and Other Dirty Movies'. We had been discussing Mediterranean culture one night after we saw *La Dolce Vita* at a film society screening. We had both told our first year classes to attend, an assignment that was thought *infra dig* and a little scandalous by some of the others. After a number of drinks, Tarrington announced that he was going to create a giant sculpture called 'The Great Tits of Ekberg', but instead he wrote the essay. Five years later, when he was able to forget how much of what he was writing came from me.

Two evenings later we played badminton, the four of us, and I noticed bruises on Madeleine's pale thigh and wondered how he had done it and whether he was prompted by Fellini's disorderly world. *Tarrington's Lust*, a sprightly Elizabethan number for the virginals.

Belle, where are you going? Don't leave. I find it reassuring to see a familiar face. Is it something I said? Unrespectful to our old pal DT, I suppose, didn't observe the old saw, *de mortuis, nil nisi bonum*. I have a brain full of Latin tags, but I can't put them all into effect. It's not to be expected. Well there, she's gone, and I regret it. It was a long long time ago that we met, when she arrived as assistant to the Dean of Arts and soon enough, because she was quick-witted and wise, became the effective Dean of Arts and stayed that until retirement, and while of course she was never paid a salary to compare to the Dean's salary, she was the brains of the office no matter which academic butterfly wore the title. When the Boat Shed opened, run by that rather sweet couple who divorced and sold it after five years, Annabelle and I were among its first customers, but now I have spoken unkindly of old Delirium Tremens, and she has remained faithful to his memory and departed. *Tarrington's Lust:* perhaps he left a bruise or two on Annabelle's firm flesh as well and she is loyal to those old wounds.

No striped ties in Madden Hall today, not one to be seen as I cast my eyes over the attentive group, smaller than yesterday's of course, but listening politely, no heckling, only Annabelle Disney's abrupt departure. Faced with the choice between me and Tarrington, she chose him, but she would always have made that choice. I wonder whether those ties belonged to the very busy or whether I am no longer under their scrutiny, having revealed myself as harmless, unlikely to call into question any matters of importance. I would like to call into question the accepted wisdom, but there is so much of it, ponderous, immoveable. I can only mark a detail here or there. I don't possess Tarrington's gift of the apparently significant phrase, the grabby oxymoron.

Moron and oxymoron. My brother was a moron – I know we don't use that word – but he had been put away and I never saw him, though I know that as a small child I was eagerly watched for signs of mental decay, but I have lasted all these years with my wits about me. I remember the occasion of his death when I was fourteen. Once, after my parents died, I thought of him, Joseph was his name, and he was long gone, and on a certain afternoon as I stood by the back window with binoculars watching an osprey hunting beyond the marsh, I thought that only I in the world was aware that Joseph had existed, that he was as close to oblivion as could be, but now I have mentioned him to all of you, though I had no such intention, and now he exists for you, and some of you are still young and sixty years from now, may recall this set of lectures – I flatter myself that such a thing is possible – and when you do you will remember Joseph and he will have as much existence as any other remembered soul. For how many years, he babbled there. No mind. Well, yes and no.

Perhaps Annabelle left us to take a windblown walk to the library and once there to use her influence and get a first peek at the Tarrington papers, to have a look at the letters I wrote to him those many years ago.

Petrus Christus. We had finished with him, I suppose. The painting is a puzzle, but so are many paintings. So in its way is the Manet I mentioned earlier. There is an odd idea abroad that art is related to beauty, and that was one of the things I liked to dispose of early in the Introduction to Civilization course. Tarrington and I would compete to see who could denounce the belief most fervently, most wickedly, and we would meet afterward for badminton and quote our good lines aloud. You see we were friends at that time. We were friends when we met on the Quai des Grands Augustins. Yes, I think we were, and the light from the river glittered among the trees, and at the back was a mirror that caught fragments of it all. That night, through some strange misapprehension, I got into a metro station after the last train and suddenly found that the lights had gone out, and I thought it too dangerous to find my way out in the dark, so I endured the night there, the odd winds and sounds, and the terrible thoughts of life ending and nothing achieved. A week later I returned to summer here and what ensued.

The van Eyck wedding picture which we have already discussed appears to be the earliest of those I plan to mention, and scholars who have chosen to comment on the use of convex mirrors in other paintings of this time and place usually describe them as something derived from van Eyck, and probably they are right, but each painter uses them in his own way. The most obscure of them is Robert Campin. Who may not be himself at all – that is, he may not be the man who painted the paintings known by his name. The wonders of scholarship. I will skip some of the historical problems as to whether Campin and the Master of Flémalle are the same man. Call him what name you wish. I have a greater problem in the fact that I have never seen the original, and can only deal with it through inadequate reproductions. It is dated just four years after the van Eyck paintings and appears to be the most directly derived from it. Campin, one would say, was no ironist, and what the convex mirror sums up is what would be expected, a back view of John the Baptist and a kneeling donor, the same scene which the painting portrays from the front, though there may be other details. Hard to make out from reproduction, a small figure perhaps, who could be the artist, an open door.

Mirror, mirror on the wall. That's the other great Disney, of course. I say that although Annabelle is not here to enjoy the reference. Mirror, mirror on the wall. I remember one night coming in late from a public lecture, and finding my wife Anne sitting naked on the bedroom floor in front of a mirror with a pencil and paper, attempting to draw herself. When I appeared in the bedroom door, she crumpled the pictures and would not show them to me, and she pulled on a dressing gown and carried them off and burned them. She wanted to see herself and couldn't, she said when she came back, and I said there was no need, for I could see her, and I drew back the fabric of the dressing gown and described what I could see, the pink, soft body, and perhaps she was pleased. I don't know whether she ever tried to draw herself again.

The donors in those early religious paintings had found a way to see themselves as part of a holy story, to combine vanity and piety. *Look at me on my knees with the saint just behind my back, the two of us reflected in the same mirror. I have paid a good sum to a master painter in order to have this done. It will hang in my house. All the things I own return me to myself, show who I am, but this more than any. John the Baptist with his beard and curls and little lamb, bare-legged, in a loose cloak, holds a book which must be a book of truth and on my knees I am attentive to that truth. You can see my seriousness in my face.* A pause for a glass of water also gives me a moment to catch my breath, stretch, perhaps assemble my thoughts. As I draw toward the end of this second talk, I confess that I understand those who need a little Dutch courage mixed with their water, something to

53

propel them the last few steps up the hill. There is no hilltop, of course, for the landscape of these lectures is discontinuous. Even the capacity of the convex mirror to catch events over a wide angle is insufficient, and of course the things captured are distorted. Welcome to the funhouse. It is some years since I have gone to a midway, so perhaps the innocent charms of the house of mirrors where you giggled at yourself stretched or compacted, where you kept discovering a new angle of the reflecting maze, are all gone by. I have seen a Ferris wheel on a distant horizon, and I'm sure that somewhere the rollercoaster still makes the timid shriek, so perhaps the house of mirrors is to be found. If so, I should take my grandchildren, but they live a long way off, and we meet only occasionally, although more often now than in the past. It was at the Canadian National Exhibition in Toronto that I saw my first house of mirrors, and I remember a moment of terror when I thought I would never escape, but would be trapped there forever watching my own small frightened face coming at me wherever I looked. I wonder if children are still scared by such things.

More water. The memory of that old terror dries the mouth. In my first year lecturing here, I carried a glass of water with me to every class because I was nervous about standing in front of all those students and thought my mouth might dry to the point where I would be left mute. I got over that soon enough and developed a glib fluency.

De mortuis nil nisi bonum. And of those who vanish, like Madeleine, what are we to say? *She was never seen again.* That is what we can say and no more. I do wish that Belle had not flown the coop. Frank Puncheon reached the end of his patience and has not appeared today, and besides we knew each other very little. Occasional badminton. A moment's chat in the coffee shop. Annabelle remembers it all, I'm sure, and that is reassuring in some ways, though she holds her own opinions, and there are many things we chose not to mention over all those years, and after her marriage to a respectable widower, we met only occasionally and in public.

Denman Tarrington is gone, and the past with him. He lies there on the tiles, and in the room beside his, a man sits waiting for a phone call and listening to the shower pouring down endlessly in the cubicle beyond the wall. The water was left running, did I mention that? It was what caused the other man to phone the front desk. Earlier, he thought he heard voices, but now the sound of the water goes on and on, and it begins to work on his nerves, which are a little rattled already. He is in New York for a job interview. The man is an accountant with a somewhat chequered past. When very young, he was arrested for possession of marijuana – he was in fact selling it, but the quantity he had on him was small enough that though he was convicted, he served only a comparatively short sentence in a prison in Washington State. When he got out of prison, he began to study accountancy, and he is quick with figures and has had some success. He has a small office in a suburb of St Louis called University City, and he lives on a pleasant street with tall trees and little traffic, but recently his wife told him she wants a divorce, and that she plans to take the two children and move to Palo Alto. She is love with someone. Everyone is in love with someone. On the day in question, our man is in New York because he has applied for a job with a firm of forensic accountants, and yesterday he went through an interview with them. He feels that the interview went well, and he is waiting impatiently for the phone call that will summon him back for a second and decisive interview, and in his state of impatience and apprehension, the continual running of water in the room next door makes him want to scream. Repeated noises will do that.

When he planned the trip to New York, he wondered about staying at the YMCA to save a few dollars. He makes money, but there's never enough, and the YMCA is connected in his mind with his Canadian grandfather who worked for the institution. In childhood, he met this grandfather at his home in Ottawa. He was a kindly man, and the memory of him is a good one. Still, our accountant decided that it wouldn't look right if he had to have messages left at the desk of the Y, not when he was trying for a New York job. Look successful. Always look successful. So he is paying for the hotel room, and the water is running endlessly just behind his head as he lies on the bed trying to be patient, and just before the phone rings, he calls down to the desk to complain. Because of his complaint, a bellman will come to the room, open it with a pass key and find the late Denman Tarrington, that prominent thinker and essayist, lying in the steam. So long DT.

Mirror, mirror on the wall. The doges tried to keep secret the technology of the wonderful Venetian mirrors with their astonishing bevelled edges, but the trick escaped and went north. The mirror was the first great advance in the technology of the self, the dominant instrument of our vanity until the camera came along. Explorers carried mirrors into those societies we no longer call primitive and created astonishment. The word mirror is related to the word mirage.

Yes, I stop more often to drink. You can tell that we are once again close to the day's conclusion. Your president waits patiently, having learned in his years of public life how not to fidget in his chair. Today's lecture will soon be done. We mark out the ends of things, the punctuations that offer relief from incoherence. We find words. *She was never seen again.* We were each trying to be Tarrington's equal in carelessness. There was a fire burning across the night. The tide was rising. Annabelle, who was there, has abandoned me on this bare gibbet.

As I totter about here, guzzling my water, there is a look of concern on the face of one of my young friends in the second row. I hope you will not take it badly that I refer to you in that way. As friends. Certain that you will tolerate my little jokes, I have adopted you, all three, and as I mentioned Annabelle and those past things, I reflected that you are now the age we were in those days, and you are living out the savage intensities of those years. Two of you are perhaps a couple, and the other is the observer or is waiting for the cure of a vanished madness. It is possible that the three of you share intricate delights and jealousies or that I misread the fashions of the time, and one of you awaits a soldier home from the wars. Forgive my intrusion. There are those who say that passion is no longer fashionable among the young, that they do it and forget. Like the province of Quebec, *je me souviens*.

The bird is about the fall to the court, but I make a long step and with a sweeping forehand swat it down the sideline.

Campin, van Eyck, Petrus Christus, and let me see who is left. Memlinc, yes, a nice artist's joke, for we are looking at a diptych, Virgin and Child in one wing, in the other the young donor, in his twenty-third year, it says. Anne was in her twenty-third year when we married. Where and how the two sections of the diptych were to be hung we can only guess, but behind the Virgin and Child is another of those convex mirrors, van Eyck's legacy, summing things up, joining, and in it we can see the Virgin's back and the donor kneeling in front of her, the figures from both panels brought together in one. A trick, a joke, call it what you will, but it bridges the contradiction of space and picture planes, and as the young donor got older, he must have been pleased to show the trick to his friends, look at me *there* and yet also *there*, like one of those movies in which an actor gets to play both twins.

The painting is in Bruges. Those of you who plan to summer in Europe can go and take a look at it, and you will have your own opinions, of course, and while you are there in that part of Europe, you can take a look at our next work, in that great maze of heaped-up masterpieces, the Louvre. Anne and I went to the Louvre just after we were married, but she tired easily in those days, her feet would swell, and she found it all overwhelming and went to sit outside while I wandered down the endless corridors, making notes. Long before the days of the glass pyramid, that was, before the hotels had been Americanized, when a toilet was still a hole in the floor somewhere down the hall. Anne didn't like Paris, and the next time I went, she spent the two weeks visiting her aunt. When I returned, the house was empty. I called, and she said she had decided to stay longer, so I was alone with my thoughts, as I had been that night in Paris.

My head is spinning, and I can't remember what I have said and not said. Lost in the hall of mirrors, I see my own distorted face, and try not to cry, to believe that I will find my way out, that my parents will be there, that all will be well. I will gather my forces for a race to the end. Tarrington lies in the steam while the man next door is picking up the phone, and we turn to Quentin Matsys. Gold again here, and no saints, though one would say that the painting must have been done under the influence of that other, for the mirror is once again set on a table so that it shows a view of what is outside.

A memory: I am in the lobby of a New York hotel, and I am surrounded by men and women from some sort of convention, all of them with those cheerful name tags, and close to me is a man whose tag reads, Hi, my name is Legion. Chances are I made that up, whether waking or sleeping. There was that business of the striped ties. I saw them, then didn't. *Ubi sunt qui apud nos fuerunt?* Where indeed. Perhaps my phone is ringing. Perhaps the ties are concealed under high-necked sweaters worn against the cold and snow that we know waits for us beyond the walls of Madden Hall.

Denman Tarrington got his name in the newspapers one last time. The badminton bird lay in the long grass, its feathers damp with dew. Feathers on a summer lawn where a neighbour's cat has torn apart a song-sparrow, the lovely long call vanished. I pick up the feathers and hide them from Anne. The dead bird lies in the grass. I will drive to the hill above the beach and with the binoculars, try for a sighting of the piping plover. Not easy to distinguish from the more common semipalmated plover or even the least plover, but with my powerful opera glasses, I can make such fine distinctions. The tides are high at this phase of the moon, and everything is flooded with the moaning salt. There is a wind in the hollow of the dunes and we feel it on our bare skin. Her skin is very pale.

Perhaps as I stand here lecturing, the phone in my hotel room is ringing over and over again. I must finish up here and go to answer it.

Quentin Matsys: *The Banker and His Wife*. This banker, we assume, will not find that his records are being sifted by forensic accountants. Double entry bookkeeping has just been invented in Italy, and it is possible that this banker possesses the two books, journal and ledger, that allow a systematic assessment of profit and loss. In our day, of course, there is something called a spreadsheet that is produced by a computer and creates the illusion of knowledge. In fact, this particular banker may only keep a pile of gold in a locked chest and judge his riches by the weight of the chest. Notional money, a trust in paper, has yet to come, and so he and his wife sit at a table while he examines the coins in front of him, weight and texture, congratulating himself on their value. There are, as you will remember, pearls on the table, and they allow the painter to show his skill in rendering shape and iridescence. The portrait of the banker, who paid for the work to be done, is an excuse for the painting of a still life. His wife, as all commentators note, has in front of her an illuminated book of prayers, but her eyes are on the pearls. That was her reason, surely, for marrying a banker. But that woman in University City is about to leave a successful accountant for the love of some adventurer in California. Love, love, love.

I am forgetting the mirror. Once again, almost a century after van Eyck's wedding portrait, there is a small convex mirror, and once again it allows the artist to show his consummate technical mastery, a perfect slice off the side of a sphere, the gleam of the texture of what is seen, the view of a window, its lines slightly distorted by the curvature of the mirror and beyond the window a corner of a building against the brightness of the sky, and below all this, in the corner of the mirror, the head of the other woman.

The Other Woman. Oh goodly melodrama of domestic life. Sacred adultery, the holy act of modern times. The shuttlecock husband, the shuttlecock wife. Of course in this painting, we only know that it is *some* other woman, and it is impossible to comprehend the meaning of this face. As with the two reflected women of Peter Christ, the meaning is for us to add. Perhaps this face is a maid, a mother-in-law, or perhaps it is another view of the banker's wife in a different hat. She couldn't make up her mind which hat to wear in the picture, so he offered, for a couple more gold coins from the pile on the table, to include her in the picture wearing both hats. Artists are ingenious and inventive creatures, and they can be tempted by gold.

The badminton bird floats down. The real bird soars. The piping plover is an endangered species, more and more rare as its breeding grounds vanish. Their nests can be swept away by storms. The tide is always rising somewhere. Brassai's Parisian mirrors always offer another angle, the face of a detached observer. The accountant from St Louis hears the phone ring and leaps up to answer it, hoping that it will give him the news he seeks. Just as he picks up the phone, he is aware that the water has been turned off in the room next door to his. Though he doesn't know it, he has been responsible for the official discovery of Denman Tarrington's body. Nor does he know that only a week later, I will be here, in Tarrington's place, offering you a few thoughts under a title which you may have found obscure at first, but are by now surely coming to understand.

Three

As I look down from this bare platform at the little loyal group of you gathered for the last of my lectures, I wonder whether there is among you the person who phoned me last night. A cruel prank. I was asleep, exhausted after a long day, dinner at the Boat Shed with your President – and thank you sir, it was a great kindness – and I was roused from sleep by the telephone ringing. Not the first time of course, and I stumbled from bed, my pyjamas tangled, and lifted the phone, though perhaps I should have known enough not to, but I did it, I lifted the phone and spoke, and there was that long painful resonant silence, and then something. I can't say exactly what it was, a voice, I suppose, but it seemed far off and blurred, the voice itself cracked and uncomfortable, as if speech was a great effort. It's true that I am growing a little deaf, that it is more difficult to separate voices from the surrounding noise and I'm sure that the highest pitches are gone, but it was more than that.

Back in bed, damp with sweat and yet shivering with cold, I tried to understand who it might be and told myself old stories all over again. The fire of driftwood in the middle of the August darkness, the sound of the waves as I walked back along the beach alone from the place where I had left her standing at the water's edge. Soon enough they were gone, all of them. Very late in the night, I remembered that I had mentioned to you these mysterious calls, oh not that many really, over the years, but they go on. It was then I realized that it must be a cruel prank, created by someone who has been sitting here listening to me. Now I look at every face staring toward me and wonder who it was.

To business. You will of course remember from our first hour J. W. Morrice living on the Left Bank, painting and drinking. It appears that in the 1890s he was in touch with a number of American artists, Maurice Prendergast, Robert Henri, William Glackens, and for a short while, there was among the group another Canadian artist. Probably you will know the name, though it is now more obscure than in the days of my boyhood. A man who was, among other things, the founder of the American Boy Scouts.

There is an astonishing story about this man's youth. He had a plan for what he wished to do with his life, and his father dismissed it, saying, No, become something important. Become an artist. That in Toronto in the late nineteenth century. It sounds unlikely enough, doesn't it? The father appears to have been an unlikely character.

The man who was there in Paris, though he was out of place and knew it, was Ernest Thompson Seton. One of the studies tells us that he was still calling himself Thompson at this time, but I think that is wrong. Thompson was of course his name. Ernest Thompson, born and brought up under that name, but his father, an Englishman who emigrated to Canada to fail at just about everything, liked to brag of their family's connection to the noble Scottish Setons, and eventually, his son took that name, and it was under that name he became known as a naturalist who wrote stories about animals and illustrated them with his own drawings and paintings. As a boy I collected his books, and my copies, some of them very early editions, are now in your library here. Unless they have been stamped *Library Discard* and tossed out. I didn't check.

When he introduced me two days ago, your president mentioned my little book, *The Carol of the Birds*, and I don't intend to repeat here all the things I said in that book about the specialized artists following Audubon. The great Audubon, who did portraits in order to make a living and find the time for his first love, the painting of birds. I once aspired to own an early edition of his book, but I never got beyond the Book-of-the-Month Club reproductions. I still have a couple of them framed on the wall of my apartment. The snowy owl is a favourite since it takes me back to a great moment of my boyhood. A lovely memory.

My dog was named Jim – I can't remember why – and this is a story of a boy and his dog. I wonder whether boys still have dogs, and whether they still attend Boy Scout meetings in church basements and learn to tie knots. It seems unlikely, but that is the world I grew up in, and I used to take my dog Jim for walks in the fields and woods on the edge of town, and we would chase rabbits and set grouse into noisy flight among the trees. In the summer, we went fishing.

When I moved here, after my years in the big cities, I began to watch birds more systematically, keeping a checklist, spending hours on the beach observing waterfowl and shorebirds. Anne was used to my habit, and it was always easy to pick up the binoculars and announce that I was driving down to the water. The pastime of a summer day, and an easy lie to tell when I began to need one.

The print of the snowy owl hangs over the desk where I work or try to work, as it has for years, as it did in the months when I was working on *The Carol of the Birds*, slides arriving, books on interlibrary loan. It wasn't an academically respectable pursuit – wildlife art is thought of as the art of the department store – but it had its roots in my early life, and it helped to assuage my loneliness in the years when I was alone in the big frame house.

Jim and I had come through a patch of woods that afternoon and through a small valley where Jim had chased a rabbit and barked at a noisy red squirrel, and on the far side of the valley was an empty field, one that was not farmed, for some reason, just long grass growing wild, with a few hawthorns here and there. Jim was far ahead of me, but I knew that when we came to the next road, we would meet up. I can't remember the season of the year, and it's not clear to me why the owl should have been there, late going north, early coming south, but suddenly and silently there it was, a large white bird, not pure white but flecked with traces of grey like shadows on snow, and it lifted itself into the air just in front of me, and I stopped, astonished and breathless. I swear there wasn't a sound as it came up in front of me, so that it was like a spectre, close to me, then gone, over the grass, into the trees and vanished.

That is a story that I tell myself, about a world where I once lived. When I got home I tried to draw a picture of the owl, but I couldn't get it right, and I'm not sure that I have got it right now, describing it to you. The very rhythm and contrivance of any sentence or paragraph is misleading. When I was young, I admired the animal stories of Ernest Thompson Seton, but if I try to read them now, they appear to me mannered and false. As an artist he is neither Morrice nor Audubon, and yet there is something touching about his survival in the face of an unpleasant and unhelpful father who lived in a world of boastful falsity, about the way he endured an unhappy marriage until his daughter was away from home.

When he was in Paris, he spent his time at the zoo, studying the animals there, those that had been bought to replace the former stock, all eaten during the siege of 1870 when the Germans blockaded the city and there was no food. *The only reasonable thing to do with our feathered friends is to eat them.* That was Tarrington's comment in a review he wrote of *The Carol of the Birds.* We were not otherwise in touch in those days, and the review was an act of malice.

It was back in those years, just after a graduation ceremony, that one of our former students appeared in my office door, one of Tarrington's regulars from his nights in the barroom. We spoke of nothing much, and then the conversation turned around and I found that he was telling me how Tarrington had paid him to keep an eye on Madeleine when hubby was away. While DT was in Paris screwing whatever he could get, this student played detective with the abandoned wife lest anyone else discover the silky texture and pearly iridescence of her skin. One of the questions I was never able to answer about Madeleine is how much of what she was developed from her own nature and how much from what Tarrington had done to her. After that conversation in my office, I knew a little more about how it had all happened, now it was too late to make anything of the knowledge. The enduring question: was it always too late? The artist's blindness makes possible the artist's vision.

Seton, who once was Thompson, is not in anyone's eyes an important artist, but just as the convex mirrors are an image of one moment of Flemish art, so his animal pictures, along with the stories they illustrate, embody a moment in the developing culture of North America. He did some fine bird studies, but his illustrations have all the annoying false drama of their kind, and in fact they are demeaning to the animals. The most impressive things, in many ways, are the incidental drawings, the illuminated title pages. In the introductions, Seton gave credit to his wife for her design of the books. He is eager to tell us that she suggested to him what to illustrate. Though there was some deep incompatibility between him and this young American woman that he met on the boat on his way to Paris, he struggled to be a devoted husband. That saddest of struggles.

Imagine a mirror not merely convex but spherical, catching everything at once. We were in a nursery where Anne wanted to look for black currant bushes. It was that last summer. Anne was just back from her extended visit to her aunt, and we had met Madeleine in a supermarket. She didn't drive, and when Anne chose to offer her a ride home, she accepted and invited us to stay for dinner. On the way, we stopped at the nursery, and while Anne looked for her black currants, Madeleine and I affected to ignore each other and wandered aimlessly. The nursery sold not only plants but garden decorations, and one of them was a little stand with a spherical mirror on top. I suppose it was intended to go in a pool or amid the flowers to catch the bright colours and reflect them back.

I stood at one side and looked at the shining sphere, and I noticed how it showed Madeleine's figure, some distance off on the other side, reflected it back to me only a little distorted, and as I watched, she turned and looked at me intently, and as she was studying me, the mirror showed Anne, who appeared from the door of a greenhouse and stopped to watch Madeleine watching me. Madeleine was wearing a very short dress that day and those Indian sandals – water buffalo, weren't they? – and her pretty legs were bare. Tarrington was still absent. The three of us were about to go to her house for dinner, and the moment hovered over those three figures, caught in a shining globe. The mirror focused all these things to a point in my brain, and I half understood the meaning of it. What I thought I understood was what I thought was freedom.

I would like to forget that telephone call last night, that voice. This morning, wanting to discuss it with someone, I tried to call Annabelle, but she was unavailable or refuses to speak to me.

He heard voices, you know, Ernest Thompson Seton. One voice, mainly. It gave him instructions about how to live his life, and he called it his Buffalo Wind. Well, he had to call it something. If I put it to you as a question, if I put it to you, Mr President, still here loyally listening, whether it seems likely that the man who founded the American Boy Scouts heard voices speaking to him – before I had told you this story, of course – I doubt that you would have expected it. That may simply go to show that we expect too little. It was also a period when many people were fascinated by these things. Spiritualism answered some need. It never dies, I suppose, that longing. There's nothing new about the New

Age. Charles G.D. Roberts, who was a professional acquaintance of Seton's – they both wrote animal stories – liked to play with ESP and horoscopes and was once visited by the ghost of a little girl.

Who had committed suicide. Some choose to return, others don't. Some bodies are never found.

In the next few years, I hope to return to the magic of my childhood, to write more about the use of animals in art, from the religious allegories of the medieval period to the work of our time, scientific in its details, escapist in its meaning. It is only as we have begun to wipe out the animal world that we have chosen to put it on our walls. We can see the meaning of anything only when we are threatened with its loss. Animal art has gone from a reflection of a new scientific taxonomy, to an expression of the earliest conservationist ideals, to sheer nostalgia, and will go beyond, soon enough, to the hysterical fear and hatred of the animal rights activists.

As I was telling you that story about Jim and the snowy owl, I reflected on how that boy became a university professor and found himself here in front of you. All accident, really, but representative. I am at one with history. My father was in charge of purchasing for a large store in a middle-sized city set among fertile farms. It would never have occurred to him or his brothers to attend a university, but by the time I completed high school, it was becoming a common thing, and so off I went. Too lazy to work, I suppose, and I did a master's degree instead and got a fellowship to go somewhere else and begin a doctorate. As the universities went on expanding, jobs fell into my lap. Tarrington was able to exploit all this, to become an adjunct to the new ruling class, while I was prepared to settle for a quiet life. I remember that when John Kennedy was elected president of the United States, Tarrington noticed that Harvard was moving to Washington and began to show an interest in all things American. His mother was American, of course, so he had one foot in the apple pie.

My favourite recipe: mixed metaphors on toast. Tarrington is toast. DT is a Library Discard. It was a couple of months ago and I was idly pressing the button on my remote and watching pictures appear and disappear when I recognized his face. It was one of those pretentious cable channels, and Denman Tarrington was generously offering his views of just about everything. A new book was being written, it appeared, about his heart attack. This was clearly a lie as Tarrington had no heart. There was a direct wire from his brain − a capable one I admit − to his penis, which, as he made clear to the deep-browed man conducting the interview, was still in a flourishing state. The book was to be called *Heart Murmurs* and was to encompass all the great themes of his oeuvre. He actually said that, and the man actually listened to him. As I watched I kept hoping that he would have another coronary infarction right there on the air, but of course, for all the fake spontaneity, the interview was taped and edited and Old DT was alive or dead somewhere else. He was about to appear, we were told, to deliver the opening public lecture at an important conference in New York. They announced the date.

Some of the problems in Seton's marriage were inherent in who each of them was. She was a city girl; he was a country boy. His earliest days were on a pioneer farm in southern Ontario, and when his father moved them to a poor area of Toronto, the small, innocent, cross-eyed boy was miserable. Birds and animals were always his greatest love, and he built himself a little cabin in the Don Valley to escape. So of course he married a woman who loved city life, and when they moved to the country imagined that their house was haunted. The ghost of a murdered musician was the story.

Anne never succeeded in meeting the ghost in our house at the edge of the country, much as she wished it. Perhaps no one had been murdered there. When we arrived, the house was still bloodless. It was, I feel sure, something less than mere chance, that when I moved out of that house, my daughter Sylvia got back in touch with me. At last she felt free to do it, and I met my grandchildren, the little Greens. She had stories to tell about the years between, about Anne's hard fate, and as I watched Tarrington's heavy, confident face smiling at the world, famous on television, I willed the clogged arteries of his heart to contract, and his body to fall from the chair to the studio floor, the producers cutting quickly to some other image. We all need someone to blame. Recall the rage of mad old Maugham.

Be patient. I will get to the point. I'm sure I will. Last night, as I lay awake after that phone call, the mind racing, as if everything in my life had to be accommodated, put in order, comprehended and forgiven in the next five minutes, I recalled that in my first lecture I had not mentioned Morrice's war paintings. Lord Beaverbrook was responsible for getting him commissioned. It wasn't his kind of subject, but he worked steadfastly enough at it. Met Augustus John, I believe, who was doing the same things. Under conscription. We all know that experience, from time to time, of being under orders from another place. We hear the orders of a voice, even if we don't call it Buffalo Farts.

Art began with animals. You have all seen versions of those cave paintings from France and North Africa. Men and women hiding in holes in the earth, suddenly felt a need to mix up red mud with water or urine or the sap of a tree and to make the world's first steps at interior decoration. If we don't count the bower bird, and that is not quite the same thing – though for all we know the man in the cave was doing it to persuade a woman huddled in a corner that he was a clever geezer, much smarter than Ugh who lived in the cave next door and was making eyes at her. It's difficult not to make jokes about people who live in caves. I grew up with a cartoon called, if I remember, Alley Oop, in which the characters were oddly shaped figures dressed in hanks of fur. I'm not sure if they had fire in the caves, or if the drawings were done in darkness or by a little glimmer of distant daylight. A blank, unmediated life, and scholars try to understand what was in the mind of the person who felt the need to record the shape of bison and antelopes. A way to control them, magic to put the prey in their power – that's one of the standard explanations, but I've heard it suggested that it was something more detached, an impulse of awe and wonder, the impulse behind all art. Not to eat it, but to know it.

Yesterday, before your president kindly took me out to dinner, I had a few minutes free and I spent them in your library, glancing at a few books on animals in art to prepare myself for today's effort. I was startled to find, on the same shelf as all the beasts, a book called *Woman as Sex Object*. I suppose the cataloguer was working in categories like Art, Subject Matter Of, and women and birds went to the same place. English slang, 1960s. And Jerome Bosch gave us lots of feathered friends in his sexy garden of earthly delights.

Everything is connected to everything else. The falcon god of the Egyptians prefigures the hawks I saw hunting over the marsh behind the Summer House. From the window where I stood at the end of that long night, watching the pale grey light that comes before dawn, when the luminescence comes up out of the ground, slowly, slowly, while in another room, my daughter was sleeping, and far off the tongue of water was luminous as pearl, the sky was empty, no hawk, and for the moment the birds were silent. I had passed the night – from the coming of darkness through standing by Madeleine watching the distant fire, to more darkness, and driving from street to street searching for Anne, finding nothing. And nothing here when I returned. Everyone was gone, and I knew it would all be changed, but I couldn't see how, not yet. Though I stood in a well-built house, I might as well have stood in a cave or on the bare desert earth worshipping animal gods, eminent and careless. Alone, we are as bare as critters huddled in a cave, making lines on the rock face.

Ernest Thompson Seton lived to be a very old man, settled in New Mexico, married to a second wife. He sired a child when he was somewhat older than I am now. A terrifying thought and not entirely credible. You can't, I'm certain, imagine me the father of a red little thing, screaming out for the comfort of its mother's breast. I am a grandfather, after all, a retired professor.

There is an entertaining story about Seton in Paris, trying to get rid of the carcass of a dog he had been dissecting. You know the sort of thing. Police searching for a murderer who may be throwing pieces of his wife's body into the Seine. Seton is trying to do the same with the body of the dissected dog. Perhaps he made it all up. Perhaps it was a dark dream. You must see what I mean.

Since animals can't be paid to hold a pose, animal art depended, at least until the invention of the camera, on the infinite patience of dead models. Audubon would wire freshly killed birds to a grid in order to produce a lifelike rendering. The illustrators of bird books all too often had to work from skins and stuffed birds in museum collections, and the colours, especially of the unfeathered areas were not always perfect. Audubon worked on a large scale and with great precision and of course always put his birds and animals in a suitable landscape, but there is a strange mock eternity to his portrayal, something of the magic stillness that catches us in naive art. His landscapes have all the ghostly precision of Henri Rousseau.

Art stops things dead. The truth shall make you free, but the facts shall make you nervous.

Over the doorway of Victoria College at the University of Toronto, it says 'The Truth Shall Make You Free'. I noticed it when I stopped in there many years ago to visit an old friend. I had been just up the street at the Royal Ontario Museum where there was a show called 'Animals in Art'. It was during the days that I was working on my little book, and the trip to Toronto was enlightening. It was a surprise to discover how many artists from how many countries were painting birds and beasts.

That trip was also the only occasion in my life when I found myself in intimate circumstances with a complete stranger, a cheerful young woman I met on the train. It's hardly a matter to be discussing from a public platform, but Victoria College says the truth shall make you free, and I've always wanted to express my gratitude. Auburn hair. Thank you, my dear. You see life doesn't end when we believe it must. It is only art that brings everything to a standstill, the fox unmoving in the snowy landscape, as if he might be that charming stuffed dog in the Victorian exhibit at the museum. When the dog passes to his reward, have him done by a taxidermist, and set him up next to your favourite chair, send him to the dry cleaners now and then.

When I was young, popular magazines offered courses in taxidermy, something you could take by mail, the ads right next to those for Charles Atlas who guaranteed to produce muscles by dynamic tension. I wonder how many young men were haunted by the fear of being the skinny goof who had sand kicked in his face by a bully, the one who would never get the girl.

You might have had Tarrington stuffed, you know, and added him to the material in the archives. The corpse would have been fresh enough, kept damp by all that warm steam from the shower. A remark in poor taste, perhaps, but it would have been in the spirit of his best work. He was after all the man who called a book *Geographies of Standing Flesh*.

He was missing from that image in the spherical mirror at the garden centre, still off in Paris, doing research. The three of us are small in that gleaming reflective surface, round as the earth, and the curve of the mirror makes the sky above look like a whirlpool of cloud spinning downward, a bright flash to one side the suddenly revealed sun. The clouds are flying by, but we are motionless as models posed for the artist to catch and record. *Johannes de Eyck fuit hic.* Kilroy was here. Tarrington was in Paris. Somewhere behind a tree, his student, the spy, watches it all, like the eye of God. Madeleine had caught him at his spying one day that summer, he told me in our later interview, and invited him into the house, and one way and another, she got the truth out of him. When I came back from Paris, I knew that something about her had changed, but I didn't know what it was. It led her to demand an account from me of Tarrington's activities in Paris. Thinking that I had my reasons, I told her.

We keep returning to Paris. When I was in New York, something strange happened to me. I had flown into Newark, and now I was in a cab, going from the Port Authority bus terminal to my hotel, and I discovered that I was speaking to the cab driver in French. Natural enough I suppose, since I had flown from Montreal, but I believe that I thought I was in Paris, though the cities don't resemble each other in the slightest, and the cab, which appeared to be falling apart and had a thick grille and glass separating me from the driver, was a dead giveaway. I spoke to the driver in competent French, he replied in what I took to be demotic Spanish and we lapsed into an appropriate silence until I reached my destination.

Nobility, perhaps ersatz nobility, is one of the features of animal art. *The Monarch of the Glen.* We portray them as noble creatures, the horses, lions, dying stags, though in one period animals got into art mostly when they lay Dutch and dead, a heap of game ready for the pot, piles of ducks and hares which must have stunk to high heaven before the artist was finished with his delicate and perfect rendering of the fur and feathers. A kind of still life, which in French is, appropriately, *nature morte.* Dead nature indeed. Still, the ospreys, nearly wiped out by DDT, are coming back. My last day here, before I moved to Montreal, I drove down to the river mouth, and then walked over the rocks to the high point that you all know, and I saw an osprey hovering there, and watched him plunge into the water and then lift himself into the air again, and of course I saw nobility in the creature's eagerness and power.

He got the job, you know, the man in the room next door to Tarrington's corpse, and that was some small consolation for the loss of his wife and children. When he picked up that ringing phone, the voice on the other end was not the office secretary, but the chief accountant himself, asking him if he was free to come back for another talk that very afternoon, and he said that he was free, and as they made the arrangements, he thought what a good thing it was that he had told them from the first interview about his marijuana conviction. They had accepted it, with a joke about all the ones who didn't get nabbed, glances from one to the other, all knowing that some of them had smoked up and probably indulged in other recreational drugs, and they were not going to punish him because he had the bad luck to get pinched. The conviction, after all, was for simple possession. Perhaps they considered that his first-hand experience of a correctional facility would give him insight into the criminal mind.

I wonder if there is such a thing as the criminal mind. The inability to postpone gratification: that's the sociologists' phrase for it. The middle class gets to where it's going by waiting to have children, by saving for a house. I am tempted to say that Tarrington never postponed a gratification in his life, but that can't be true, can it? He wrote those books when he might have been drinking or chasing women, and I have wondered from time to time if his relentless appetite wasn't a pose, tough talk from a good hard-working Canadian boy. Perhaps he lied to me in Paris. He might have been spending all his time at the Bibliothèque Nationale, and I passed on the lie to Madeleine, and she opened the vodka bottle and prepared herself for revenge. The truth shall make you free.

There is a terrible animal painting by George Stubbs, terrible in the old sense, instinct with terror. *Lion Devouring a Horse*, it's called, and it's found in the Tate Gallery. The lion is on the horse's back, its teeth and claws sunk into the flesh, and the horse, a powerful creature, white, with a pure white mane and tail, twists its neck in desperation, its big teeth trying to reach toward the cat that is destroying it. The scene, of course, comes not from anything seen – though there are rumours that Stubbs observed such an unlikely event in Italy – but from artistic precedents and the mind of the painter. Stubbs was a painter both workmanlike and brilliant who started out as a student of anatomy and lectured on the subject to medical students and made his living as a painter of horse portraits for the aristocracy. Stubborn and self-assured, a north country workman, yet he must have had terrible dreams. Perhaps it was the love of horses that made him wish to see one in such a moment of extremity, the throat strained, the mouth open, the eyes wide. Such things occur in the imagination of every man.

My young friends in the second row are back – all but one – and they are questioning that last word. I said man and meant man. I cannot imagine that a woman would paint such things, though perhaps you have your own vision of *terribilità*. I have caught glimpses, but it is not the same, or not yet. Perhaps men and women will come to share the same nightmares. I look down at all the faces that watch my performance, and I have no idea what lies behind them. Setting out the menu for dinner. Making plans to write a book review already overdue. Wishing I would finish so you can get to the nearest toilet. Wondering what your lover is up to at this moment. At least no one is sleeping today. The dozy have departed, gone to nap elsewhere.

In my first lecture, you will remember, I reflected on the

79

flavour of the Edwardian world and the figures who populated it, not quite Victorian, not quite modern, and Ernest Thompson Seton was another of them. A decent upright man, no doubt, who thought that woodcraft could keep boys out of trouble, and idealized his picture of the Indian brave. He proved to his wife that the ghost in their isolated house in the country was only the sound of wind through broken glass – that was the song of the murdered musician. He went for long walks in the country, and the sickly boy who heard voices lived on into his eighties and sired a child not long before the end. Yet he liked to draw wolves, was drawn to the ferocity of predators, the sharp teeth and the snarling over the bare bones of what they devour. The natural world lives on flesh, and the hawks I watched crossing the marsh were hunting for what they could kill. There is something a little theatrical about the wildness of his wild creatures.

Anne and I stood in the yard with that marsh beyond us and beyond that the sea. We stood on the lawn that was full of dandelions and small clover flowers and swatted the badminton bird back and forth, pretending there was a net. We had been to the beach that day, and Anne's legs – her pale pink skin very sensitive to the sun – were reddened with a sunburn that would keep her awake during the night, and in the dark, I would get up and find a bottle of baby oil and rub it tenderly into the burnt skin, my fingers noticing the gentle curve of the flesh, the whiteness of the round belly. Pink roses and the white.

Whiteness, the white horse being devoured by a lion, the white swan, the captive unicorn in a field of flowers. When Anne looked in the mirror in our bedroom, hoping to draw what she observed, she couldn't see herself. The mirror was empty. It was fastened on the inside of the closet door, and when I sold the house I left it, but it has no mind to remember what it saw.

I sip water and reconsider. There are medieval manuscripts with accurate drawings of birds, and the illuminations in many of them show what appears to be accurate observation of the natural world. The commonplace would have it that the world was entirely symbolic in those days, an allegory of faith, every creature in the bestiary a myth complete with inaccurate biology, the phoenix, the pelican wounding its breast to feed its young, and yet in the middle of this, some monk had looked at a chaffinch and knew what it was like, so that the little bird in the corner of a manuscript is as lively as any on a branch in the woods. Pisanello and his circle produced birds in the same loving detail as Audubon. Observation preceded taxonomy and curiosity is always with us. Seton raised young prairie chickens and found that the dance they do was innate, hard-wired as we would say now. 'The Hard-Wired Prairie Chicken Dance.' Sometimes I have thought that Tarrington's essays began as titles and he then had to invent material to go along.

In New York recently, I stood in the Metropolitan Museum and looked at a remarkable horse painting by Rosa Bonheur, purchased in 1887 for a goodly sum by Cornelius Vanderbilt. Yes, I will come back to Rose Happiness.

I had intended to mention that the earliest known work by George Stubbs is eighteen plates illustrating a book on a new system of midwifery, the artist intruding on the privacies of parturition. He was always fascinated by anatomy, having that earnest application to fact and enquiry that came along in his time and brought us the spinning jenny and Josiah Wedgwood. Stubbs produced figures for Wedgwood, and in spite of all his seriousness and hard work, he ended his life in want. I have not seen those plates of women torn open to give birth. Nowadays every father observes the thing he put in there being expelled into real life, but I didn't. I was presented with Sylvia when she had been licked into shape. The bestiary again.

'Applied Anatomy: The History of Sexual Advice.' You will all have read that one, I'm certain. That one got him on the television to boast about his own sexual prowess. I tried to avoid hearing about it, but for a few weeks, Tarrington was ubiquitous, and I was forced to imagine what he did and who he did it to. Lies, all lies, as likely as not, or so I persuaded myself. All the business about tantric yoga and female submission.

I have a plan for the money I am being paid for giving these lectures – yes, I am being paid, and handsomely too, I must confess, though I suspect they sliced a little off the original offer made to the Great and Famous. You needn't look embarrassed, Mr President, it's only to be expected. Save a little from this year's share of the endowment and next year you can go to the very top. My plan is to go to Paris and to spend my days in the Louvre, to document, for my own purposes, every picture of possible use to me. The horse paintings of Delacroix, for example. It is some time since I have been to Paris, and I understand that the city is plagued by an epidemic of upscale boutiques. You might as well be in Toronto, people say, but I'm sure the river is still there, and the trees and the gold stone of the old buildings. I will sit by the Medici fountain and watch the lovers. I am too old to postpone gratification.

My voice is growing a little hoarse, as you can hear. Three days of shouting in the acoustic horror that is Madden Hall. I remember when concerts were held here, but the musicians objected and finally they were transferred to St. Paul's, just down the block. There the musicians complained about the smell of incense. Musicians are chronic complainers. Men and women are chronic complainers. Things are never what they were or what they could be. A kind of vision, I suppose, to be stricken by possibility, an appetite for life expressed in dissatisfaction, a No which is a Yes, and better to be articulated, set out in vivid words than stifled into a mere energyless silence, though every complaint is beside the point, is only the approximate notation of what is missing.

Notation: it's been pointed out that every artist has a way of painting an eye, a nose, a mouth, his own shorthand of strokes. Stubbs painted his horses on a large scale, with a careful sense of the musculature, that love of anatomy and the ways things work. The man I began with, J. W. Morrice, saw horses as working creatures, part of the city, whether Montreal or Paris, and he had a quick, accurate way of painting a horse, a few strokes and the shape was there among the other shapes, a coloured object among the other coloured objects. He drank, perhaps because the effect of alcohol was to make the sheen of the surfaces more intense; meaning and expectation gone, and what was left was pure notation, the love of paint. A kind of ontology, pure present. That's the reason that music is only music in fragments, set free from time.

Have I made clear how very thin those pieces of wood are, on which Morrice did his sketches? Fragile, and sometimes very dark, as if the picture were half a secret. The little portrait of Léa Cadoret in the shade of trees, all shadowy greens: he would tell and not tell. Each time I leave the Musée des Beaux Arts after examining those small mysterious things, I climb on the homeward bus, number 24, and I am taken west along Sherbrooke Street. At certain times of day, the bus passes a number of schools, and adolescent boys and girls stand by the edge of the road and some come aboard. There was a day when I sat by the window, and looking out, I saw two girls in school uniforms, short kilt, long socks, white blouse, one of them tall and a little gangly, the other short, almost plump. Their faces were turned away from me, but I knew if they turned I would know them, Anne and Madeleine come back to haunt me, starting life again at the place on the great wheel marked Youth while I am trapped in the seat marked Age.

83

Say that with a long sweeping stroke I have lifted the bird so high over the court that it is hard to make out whether it is a shuttlecock or a chickadee flying from tree to tree. Watch its slow eternal descent.

Living here, you will all have watched the tide coming in, the moment-by-moment encroachment across the beach, or the slow rise over the rocks. The whole ocean is tilting toward you, with all the power of those tons of water, and you know that nothing can stop its arrival, nothing can hold it back. Far along the beach, we can see the fire of driftwood, and the shapes of men and women close by moving out of darkness and into darkness. Annabelle Disney was there somewhere, but today she is not available to give her testimony. She is an absent witness, if a witness at all. She was one of those figures far off by the fire as we stood by the edge of the water. *She was never seen again.* The night smelled of salt, and as we stood among the dunes, I felt the eyes watching us, turned away and walked back toward the burning driftwood.

I expect that the striped ties will return for the end of the last lecture, since they were here for the beginning of the first. Their pattern of presence and departure is unreadable, but all truth is unreadable until it is the heap of dead facts we call history. Sometimes I have flattered myself with the thought that all the best of Tarrington's essays, the ones that made him famous, grew out of our conversations, and when I have that thought, I have to admit that I would never myself have written them. The ideas would have vanished into time. There was a balance of forces in the days when we were here, like one of those very close games of badminton when the bird sailed to every corner of the court, and as I stood off the back corner and drove it down the line, I could see Anne in front of me, leaning forward on her toes, her tidy sweet body all on the alert, Madeleine, her eyes wide, watchful, breakable, and Tarrington's bearded face and simian arms coiled into a ball of ferocity ready to strike out. In later years, his essays were excessive, full of empty gestures as he went on from woman to woman searching for death or the perfect American orgasm.

North America is many things, none of them comfortable. Though Ernest Thompson Seton idealized life in the wilds, it was nearly the death of him when he was a boy. His health had collapsed and he was sent to spend the summer with a farmer near Fenelon Falls. The whole family came down with malaria, and in a state of hallucination he imagined giant snakes coming after him. Odd how these invalid boys live almost forever. He survived to become one of the important figures in the discovery of Nature with a capital N. It was in those years that the great parks were being created, Banff and Jasper, Yellowstone and Yosemite, imaginary wilderness preserved as the continent gave in to civilization.

Now the surface of the moon is covered with garbage. Every little picture store has prints of foxes and geese, perhaps an eagle or even a wolf. It has something to do with the nature of sentimentality, how we adulate what we destroy, like Ugh-the-caveman's jealous neighbour scratching out an antelope in red ochre and then setting off to bring one down.

It was probably an attempt to escape any taint of sentimentality that led Audubon to draw birds at exactly life size, big big, small small. He had the scientist's regard for accuracy, and this may be the source of the haunted quality of his work. His birds symbolize nothing, and they are both alive and dead. Corpses posing as living birds, as if Denman Tarrington had been stuffed and set up on the stage here in a chair to listen to my remarks about him.

Water, water.

To begin again. Strange stories cling to the reputations of the famous, and scholarship has the job, pleasing to the puritan, of scrubbing off the encrustations of myth. Audubon had the habit of inventing new biographies, especially the stories of his early life, not the first or the last artist to do it, for they all grow confused over what happened as opposed to

85

what ought to have happened. Surrounded by memories as I stand here, I have given you gratuitous and probably tiresome glimpses of my own past life, and not being an artist, I have been limited to the events, but I might have invented a larger story, opaque and splendid, myself as hero or antihero. Concerning Audubon, somehow the tale got about that he was the lost Dauphin, Louis xvii, the King of France in disguise paddling down all the rivers of North America looking for rare birds.

There were a few Audubon prints in my now lost collection of slides. They used to be very popular. As I said, my copies came from the Book-of-the-Month Club − my mother belonged − but they have been replaced in public favour by more contemporary animal pictures, slick, silent things.

My slides are still, I suppose, lying on the floor of a cab somewhere in Montreal. When I return there, if I can remember the name of the cab company, I will phone and try to reclaim them, though what earthly use they will be, I can't think. I doubt that I will receive another such invitation. There will not be another sudden death. Surely not. When the phone in my apartment rings, it will be the ophthalmologist's secretary reminding me to come in for another test, or it will be someone who wishes to do a survey of my shopping habits or a young man speaking elegant French who wishes to sell me a subscription to *Le Devoir*. Or it will be another of the silent caller's silent calls.

Last night was surely a prank or a delusion. Perhaps it was a dream. After all these years of waiting for a voice to speak, the obsession has gone deep and returns as a nightmare. There are periods of months and years when nothing occurs but the usual wrong numbers. It is possible to achieve a small moment of enlightenment from a wrong number. The Thérèse or Raymond who is being sought has a momentary being, something known, and it is not altogether unlike the moment − watch carefully now as I shuffle the cards − when I was in your library looking at a small shelf of books on animals in art and found myself looking at something called *Woman as Sex Object*. Of course you may take this, especially my friends in the second row – and I can't help wondering why your other colleague isn't here, whether she is the most easily offended, the most easily bored, or whether she has some personal tragedy to accommodate – you will take this as a typical inappropriate joke from an old sexist. Well, so it may be, but the book was there, and whatever we legislate about the connection of man and woman, it is true that the cataloguer – another sexist perhaps – contrived to place the book on that shelf, and it is also true that artists have stared at women and noted each detail, that they have liked nothing better than to undress female persons and record the texture of flesh, not beauty but the pure phenomenon. Tarrington observes in one of his essays that Delacroix's *Lion Hunt* and Rubens' *Rape of the Daughters of Leucippus* show a similar frenzy, a similar tormenting of the posed or imagined bodies. A note on historical iconography: in the movies I see these days, the act is mostly performed with the woman on top. Make what you will of that. The spirit of the time expresses itself in a myriad of odd ways. Who is not its master becomes its slave. Madeleine was ahead of her time.

We are coming toward an end. The usual signal, my dry mouth, the glass too often emptied and refilled. A lurching gait. I am watching for the appearance of a striped tie, which will be a signal. He takes the clip-on out of his pocket, bends as if to cough and fastens it on. That will be enough. The end will come. Some of you have been with me for all three hours, not just your president who must as a part of his official duties. I'll set you free, dear Mr P. Tomorrow you will be on your own, and so will I. After the lecture, I will return to the motel room, where Delirium Tremens would have stayed if he had survived to give this series of talks. Perhaps he would have taken back with him a fresh young thing he'd picked up

87

in the course of his time here. Myself, I will return there along the snowy road, and I will look in the mirror and fail to see, as always, the meaning of what has happened. It will be the same face, the face I deserve, as Orwell put it. In the unicorn tapestries at the Musée de Cluny, the young lady shows the unicorn his face in the mirror and he appears to accept it with a certain self-satisfaction. The unicorn may or may not belong in a consideration of animal art. Less animal, more symbol. Tidy, white and one-horned. I saw the horn of a unicorn once, in an English cathedral, part of the collection of wonders.

When I get back to Montreal, the cheque will go to the bank, and I will phone and make reservations for a flight to Paris. Where we began, Tarrington and I at one café, Morrice and Ernest Thompson Seton at another, or perhaps not, perhaps it was the same one, the mirror at the back catching both moments with its perfect equanimity. There ought to be a riddle about the mirror which sees everything and knows nothing. Maybe there is.

That young woman I overheard in the library may by now have made the decision about the tattoo her lover wants. Roses on her butt. The skin reddened from the piercing, as if from a sunburn. I understand that tattoos can be painful, but I suppose that is the point; the marks left by suffering have an extra meaning. That and the permanence; you can't change your mind and get a divorce from a tattoo. Sign for a tattoo parlour: Flowers That Won't Die Till You Do – Something More Permanent Than Love. I never saw the young woman's face, but I imagine her in a certain way, and when I do I think how very young she is. At that age I was still preoccupied by the death of my dog Jim, though I didn't admit that to my undergraduate friends. We were all learning to be witty and untouched.

I hear the slow humming of the universe expanding all around us. I can posit, as everyone does now, an alternative universe in which I looked in a convex mirror and saw, close up, distorted, my own young face, and behind me at an oblique angle, just caught in the corner, someone else, a pale figure almost too small to make out, and seeing this, I understood it. A very different universe.

When he retired from the YMCA he took up gardening. He would work there in the little yard even on rainy spring days, coming in full of aches and pains, but consoled by the richness of the earth, by the way things grew where he planted them. It wasn't a fancy garden, a couple of roses, flowering annuals – just like those the robbers used to stifle Uncle Pumblechook – irises and peonies and delphiniums, the usual old-fashioned things along with a few green onions and radishes for salads. He often thinks of the son who died at Dieppe, though the thoughts are momentary, stray memories, an awareness of a boy he once knew, a boy standing by a bicycle with a cigarette in his mouth, his eyes half closed against the smoke.

Back in Montreal, when I have rushed to deposit the cheque lest you change your minds and stop payment, I will hurry down to the Musée des Beaux Arts on Sherbrooke to make my homage to the Morrice collection, to reassure myself that the paintings are unchanged, untouched by my words. They will be on display and just as before, but there is always the worm of doubt, the possibility that commentary has altered them for the worse, made them flatter, more obvious.

I said I would return to the horses of Rosa Bonheur. Rose Happiness kept a lion, wore trousers and smoked cigarettes. It all sounds like George Sand as played by Merle Oberon in that movie about Chopin. I was young when I saw that, and was quite smitten by her for a while. Trying to decide what a woman should be like, and here was a new version. Rose Happiness kept a lion. When I was in New York, just before I left, I stopped at the Metropolitan Museum, almost as if I knew I would be called on to come here and speak to you. I

89

looked at a few things, and the last of all was her great horse painting. Eight feet tall it is and twice as long. Creating it must have been like painting the side of a house with a half-inch brush.

The story is that she visited abattoirs to see the bodies of her subjects flayed, and her love of horses and knowledge of them comes out in the painting on Fifth Avenue, the tremendous musculature of the shoulders and thighs, the wild eyes of the white one in the middle of the herd that is being directed into a paddock by a handful of men, the power of the beasts under their control. Rose Happiness sees their splendour but she is not maddened by it. Perhaps she knows why women and animals are on the same shelf. She kept a lion and her speciality was the painting of wild creatures.

Look, there it is, the first of the ties has returned. Time to stop. One more glance at the vast canvas of Rose Happiness, that vision of great and mastered horses, and I leave the museum.

Born in Ontario, David Helwig attended the University of Toronto and the University of Liverpool. He taught at Queen's University, worked in summer stock, was literary manager of CBC Television Drama, did a wide range of freelance writing and has authored more than twenty books. His most recent work is a novel, *The Time of Her Life* (Goose Lane, 2000), and a collection of poetry, *This Human Day* (Oberon Press, 2000).

David Helwig currently lives on Prince Edward Island. He has indulged his passion for vocal music by singing with choirs in Montreal, Kingston and Charlottetown.